"The shei
precisely

Marti Holland heard these words and froze. A moment later she jumped up from her seat and skirted the column behind her—but no one was there.

Had she imagined that deep-timbred voice? She looked around. The delegates' lounge at the United Nations was quiet. Perhaps she had dozed off and dreamed it all.

Marti ran toward the elevator in time to see two men disappearing into it. For some unknown reason she associated the resonant voice with the tall, sandy-haired man. Just then the elevator doors closed. She had to find a security guard—and fast!

ABOUT THE AUTHOR

Eve Gladstone believes that romance and
adventure are a constant challenge, and
Checkpoint marks her second foray into
Intrigue. Since she began her writing career,
she has had a number of books published,
both fiction and nonfiction. Eve lives in a
New York City suburb with her husband and
a compatible assortment of dogs and cats.

Books by Eve Gladstone

HARLEQUIN INTRIGUE
23–A TASTE OF DECEPTION

These books may be available at your local bookseller.

CHECKPOINT

EVE GLADSTONE

Harlequin Books

TORONTO • NEW YORK • LONDON
AMSTERDAM • PARIS • SYDNEY • HAMBURG
STOCKHOLM • ATHENS • TOKYO • MILAN

To Lillian Gladstone
and Gerry Melot.

Harlequin Intrigue edition published September 1986

ISBN 0-373-22049-9

Chapter One

Dusk and the wintry quiet seemed to come from a sudden holding of a collective breath. What was that bit of patter they used to intone when she was a child? "Rain, rain, go away, come again another day"?

The delegates' lounge on the second floor of the UN General Assembly Building was an enormous, high-ceilinged affair. Decorated in leathers and earth tones, everything about the place was giant sized, from the tangle of schefflera leaves in huge pots to the soft-toned paintings and hangings on its walls.

The woman at the window gazing at the river traffic below wore a bright red suit that brought out the warm brown color of her lustrous, shoulder-length hair. She was slender, of medium height, with green eyes shaded by dark lashes. There was a bridge of freckles across her nose, although the summer sun she longed for would burn her skin easily enough. Standing there in that tremendous space with its sepulchral silence, Marti Holland hugged her arms and shivered, feeling very small and alone.

Where the devil was Terry?

Marti wondered if her friend had forgotten their date. Couldn't blame her at all if she had. Perhaps they'd been to one diplomatic affair too many. The same people, the same polite, inscrutable smiles, the same bland food. On more than one occasion Marti had longed to stick a rose between her teeth and dance a fandango.

Tonight's reception was being given by the Moroccan Mission at six-thirty in the delegates' dining room on the fourth floor. Marti was tired, however, and expected to run out after a handshake with the ambassador and a turn around the room.

She glanced at the darkened sky and the low, scudding clouds moving across it. All day it had looked like rain, a portentous late-October rain that boded no good.

Marti sighed. It had been that kind of day all around: tedious, long and fruitless, with a sense of a storm about to break even in the smallest conference room. She sat as an adviser on the economic subcommittee of the U.S. Mission. A meeting with the delegates of a dozen Third World countries had taken up the entire afternoon, although nothing more had been discussed than the matter of proper seating. They would perhaps get down to business tomorrow morning, after protocol had been established. Perhaps.

Marti was scheduled to give a paper she had spent weeks preparing—a paper filled with facts and figures concerning the economics of postcolonial farming on the African subcontinent.

A barrel of laughs. If only numbers were wishes and wishes came true, what a wonderful world it would be.

Marti, whose life at that moment seemed as dry and dull as the statistics she studied, all at once wanted to break out of the window, to go floating down into the churning river and be borne far away. Where was the Marti Holland who had grown up wild and reckless two miles from here? The Marti Holland who had once used Manhattan as her playground and vowed to grab the world by the throat and give it a good shaking?

Lost in numbers, maybe, in meetings, maybe, in that elusive world that had somehow got away from her. No use thinking about it.

She was thirty-two years old, and where had it all gone?

Another glance at her watch. Six-twenty. Five more minutes, definitely no more than five. *Relax,* she told herself.

Of course, the scenario had already been written as far as Terry Atwater was concerned. She'd rush up at the last minute, breathlessly explaining that someone or something had held her up, expecting and receiving forgiveness.

Marti, on the other hand, was right on the button, having shaped her life into a meticulous daily schedule with not a second to spare. The other Marti, the Marti of ten years ago, had juggled time without worrying about where it crashed. Oh, there was plenty of it to waste, and such fun while she was at it.

Have a seat, Marti. Relax, Marti.

Next to one of the interior supporting columns of the glass building was a soft, inviting leather chair. Marti slipped into it and settled back to wait. The thick square column blocked her view to the right, but from where she sat, she could survey the lounge and keep an eye on the entrance almost directly ahead.

The activity in the lounge was as subdued as ever; secrets floated silently off into the vast, open space. That was why Marti was startled when she heard a deep masculine voice quite close to her ear. She looked around, but her nearest neighbors were two seated women conversing quietly.

There was no one else whose voice would reach her so clearly. It had to be someone on the other side of the column, she decided. The speaker was conversing in French, his accent noticeably not native.

"You can raise all the objections you want to, my nervous friend, but it can be done. Anything can be done—any time, anyhow, anywhere. All you need is a game plan and willpower. That's how we've survived all these years, in case you've forgotten. Speed, intelligence and never taking no for an answer. And for every problem I guarantee you a solution."

There was a murmured response in French. Marti couldn't catch the words.

It was some little pocket of air, some acoustic oddity that allowed the beautiful resonant voice to bounce off the window and back at her. Marti was about to get up, to let them see she was there, but the next words, spoken again in that deep timbre, froze her.

"The sheikh will die here at the United Nations precisely as planned, and you can make of that what you will."

Although she was on her feet at once, for a long moment Marti was paralyzed into inaction. When she stirred herself at last, it was too late. She skirted the column only to find that there was no one on the other side.

Had she been hearing things, a remnant of someone else's thoughts made more real than real? She looked hurriedly around. The lounge was quiet. No one stirred. Nothing ominous hovered in the air. Perhaps she had dozed off and dreamed it all.

But no, she hadn't. She knew what she had heard, and whoever had spoken those devastating words was no longer there.

A dozen people swooped into the lounge in a body, cutting off her view of the elevator. She recognized them as delegates who must have just come from a meeting. They were gesturing broadly and talking rapidly in English. There was laughter. Several people got into each other's way and apologized with much shoulder touching and smiles.

"Marti!" One of the delegates waved and beckoned her over.

"See you upstairs," she said hastily, afraid of being detained with chatting. She ran toward the elevator in time to find two men disappearing into it. One was tall and broad shouldered, with sandy-colored hair. He wore a well-tailored suit of tan plaid; she could not see his face. The other, a smaller, stockier man in a dark suit, had moved too quickly for her to take in much more than his height. The doors closed before she could signal the operator to wait.

"Damn." Marti angrily jabbed the call button.

The elevator was on its way up. It bypassed the third floor and stopped at the fourth. There was a good chance that they were getting off at the delegates' dining room, where the Moroccan reception was being held. She considered racing for the escalator and heading them off.

Breathlessly Marti looked over at the guard who stood beside the entrance to the delegates' lounge. She found him watching her sideways out of careful eyes. Of course, the guard. She expelled a sigh of relief and went quickly over to him. Proper procedure. Report at once to a guard. Let him handle it.

"Excuse me," she began a little timidly.

The guard looked down from what to her was a disconcertingly great height, keeping his walkie-talkie close to his ear. "Excuse me, but I just heard the most extraordinary conversation," she went on. "I thought I ought to…well… Did you see those two men who just got into the elevator?"

He squinted, scrutinizing her carefully. "Two men?"

Marti suddenly found herself on the defensive. He stared at her as though she were an alien being. "Right," she forged on. "Two men. They just got on the elevator. You won't believe this, but they were plotting to kill Sheikh Hikmat." The words, once out, sounded so bizarre that her sense of urgency momentarily deserted her.

The guard's eyes glinted. Softly he spoke a few words into his walkie-talkie, all the while watching her. "Now," he said severely in an accusatory tone, "who were these two men?"

He was doing his duty, perhaps even hoping that her report was true, but not quite trusting her. "I haven't the faintest idea. I told you," she repeated, impatience creeping into her voice, "they got on the elevator and went up— to the reception on the fourth floor." She stopped, momentarily drawing her lips together. "At least," she continued more slowly, "I suppose that's where they went. I don't know where else—"

The guard held up his hand. "I've called for help. Wait right here. We'll need you as a witness. Did you say you don't know who they are?" he added as an afterthought.

"I'm not even certain—" She broke off. In fact, she had no idea who they were, where they had gone or whether indeed they might not still be in the delegates' lounge. "I don't know a thing about them, just that . . . they were speaking French," she went on haltingly, "but with an accent, perhaps British. And one of them said the most extraordinary thing." The guard continued to listen impassively, his gaze roaming the corridor and lounge beyond, then settling back on her. By the very blankness of his expression she knew he was having trouble believing her.

Marti dragged in a deep breath and then let the words explode. "I'm not deaf. I was standing in the delegates' lounge, and by the oddest quirk of acoustics, I actually heard them talking about how it was possible to kill Sheikh Hikmat right here at the United Nations. He's due two weeks from now to— Look," she interrupted herself, impatient with her own confusion, "I'm going to repeat the words exactly as I heard them. One of the men said quite plainly, 'The sheikh will die here at the United Nations precisely as planned.' Those are the words exactly."

"In French?"

"Yes. And no, I was not hearing things. I understand French."

"You're sure it was Sheikh Hikmat they were talking about?"

Marti took an involuntary step back. "Yes, well, of course! Who else? No," she admitted, "the truth is, I . . ." *just took it for granted,* she finished to herself. She felt the faintest traces of a blush cross her face. Paranoia during the general session usually ran high. She was certainly subject to it as much as anyone. "Look," she added, "it's stupid to stand here and talk. We have to find them now, before they get away. Too much time has been lost already."

"We'll have someone here in a minute." A vague look of disapproval crossed the guard's face, as though Marti herself had done something wrong. "If you'll just be patient, miss, we'll take care of everything."

"They went upstairs, maybe to the Moroccan reception," she repeated softly, delineating the facts to herself. She looked around and found the elevator doors opening. "Oh, good! Wait, the operator should know something."

"Miss . . . !" the guard called after her.

Marti rushed over, stepping inside the crowded elevator along with two or three other people. "Could you hold it for just a second?" she asked the operator. But the door had already closed behind her, and the elevator was on its way down.

"Look, it's a matter of life and death," she said to the operator in an undertone. "Two men got on when you went up. One was tall, light haired; he was wearing a tan suit. The shorter one with him was in a dark suit."

The operator eyed her curiously. "Life and death, did you say?" he announced in a loud voice, as though slender women with thick brown hair and green eyes had no business discussing life and death. He drew the elevator to a stop on the floor below. Several people glared at her as they stepped off. Others pushed their way on.

Marti angrily planted herself in the door. "Just tell me what floor they got off on."

"Everybody got off on the fourth. Is that all? What do you mean, life and death?"

"Thank you." She stepped out and raced for the escalator, which would get her to the fourth floor much faster than either elevator. There she would point out the assassins to a guard, and then she'd wash her hands of the whole affair. Good heavens, what a mess to find herself in, and with everyone so damned intractable!

Still, adrenaline had her pulses racing, and she felt oddly high, as though the wish of a few minutes earlier, that she break free of the unwavering regimen of her life, had given breath to the deed.

She glanced at her watch when she arrived on the fourth floor. Six thirty-one. *Time flies when your adrenaline is high,* she noted. She went quickly around to the delegates' dining room, pulling up short at the door. The reception was already in progress. The Moroccan ambassador was standing in the receiving line along with his wife and several other members of the mission.

Security was tight. She spotted several guards but hesitated over having to repeat the story to an unbelieving stare. Her hand went automatically to the name tag pinned to her red suit jacket that identified her as Marti Holland of the U.S. Mission. Then, as she fished in her bag for her invitation, Marti felt an unreasoning panic that she had forgotten it. No, there it was, a slightly creased embossed card.

What next? Marti peered through the doorway that led into the plant-filled dining room, where the tables and chairs had been removed so that there would be plenty of space for guests. It was already crowded. There would be no easy way of finding her quarry.

There was an L to the right that led to yet another large room. Perhaps he was there—the sandy-haired man. She had no idea why she matched the beautifully timbred voice with broad shoulders and sandy hair, but she did.

The elevator doors opened, and a crowd came tumbling out. All at once Marti found herself propelled along past the guards and toward the receiving line. There was no turning back now; it would be entirely too rude. And there was one good thing going for her: as far as she knew, this was the only public entrance to the dining room. If the men had gone in this way, it was this way they'd have to come out.

She felt a warm, intimate touch at the back of her neck. Ian Levitan, who was an economist with the Australian Mission, gave her a broad, boyish grin. "Hello, love. Waiting for me?" He was a big, handsome man with a wife and a half-dozen children in New Jersey.

"Where's Mrs. Levitan?" she asked, not at all angry but pretending she was.

"She detests these things; you know that, Marti."

"No, she doesn't. You just make it uncomfortable for her by flirting outrageously with the likes of me."

"If you look luscious, you're going to have to take the consequences."

"Tell that to your wife, not to me."

"Ouch." He gave her neck a squeeze and laughed.

"Ouch is right." The line shifted forward, and Marti moved impatiently along with it, straining to catch a glimpse of the action in the dining room.

"What are you looking for?" Ian asked. "You'll get there."

"No, it's not that," she said. "Listen, Ian, I just heard—" She stopped, wondering if she should tell him. Swiftly she decided that there was no argument against doing so. Overhearing an assassination plot wasn't the sort of event one kept to oneself. Certainly the more people who knew about it, the less likely it would come about.

"Speak up, love," Ian prompted.

"I know you're not going to believe this," she rushed on, "but I just heard the most amazing thing—by mistake, I mean—in the delegates' lounge. Now, try not to treat me as if I've gone mad."

"You haven't gone mad, love, but your color's a little off. What's up?"

"I just heard someone planning to kill Sheikh Hikmat."

He gave her a look of disbelief. "Want to run it by me again?"

"You heard me right the first time."

"You were eavesdropping on someone's conversation," he stated. "Is that it?"

"I wasn't eavesdropping, Ian. As a matter of fact, I was just about to let them know I was there when I heard the words."

"What words?"

"'The sheikh will die here at the United Nations precisely as planned.'"

Ian raised an eyebrow. "People don't plot murder in the delegates' lounge, even as much as I've wanted to on occasion. It would be bad form. And they'd be overheard." He gave her a quizzical look, realizing he'd just supplied the answer to a question he hadn't quite asked.

"It was some sort of acoustical fluke, Ian; really it was."

"Did you tell anyone?"

"The guard."

"And?"

"And it's a long story," she said.

Ian gave her a slight push forward. She was at the head of the line now. "Tell me about it right after," he instructed in a whisper.

"Right." Another step and Marti found herself looking into the tiredly smiling eyes of the ambassador, a slender, handsome man who pressed her hand firmly, as though he were genuinely pleased she had come.

"So glad you invited me," Marti murmured.

To his wife, a dark-haired, somberly groomed woman, Marti made an equally vague remark, then passed on to the two next-ranking members of the mission.

In a few more seconds Marti found herself standing alone in the crowded dining room, which smelled of perfume and food and liquor. She was sorry that she had said anything to Ian. He was curious, the way a gossip is curious, but he'd want to be a hundred miles away from any possible trouble that might ensue from such knowledge.

Ian called out to her. She moved quickly into the crowd in order to escape him. It didn't matter that he was with the Australian mission and as equally committed to peace in the Middle East as she.

She had to find her quarry first, and then act. If she had to call down the entire party on the sandy-haired man's head, she would. Meanwhile, judging from the size of the crowd, finding him and his accomplice wouldn't be easy.

"Hey, where the hell were you?" A smiling Terry Atwater was making her way through the crowd. Like Marti, she worked for the U.S. Mission, but as a public liaison officer. She was tall and flamboyant in appearance, with a fountain of jet-black hair parted in the middle, friendly amber eyes and a full, bright red mouth. She greeted Marti with a loud kiss that just missed her cheek. "I waited a full fifteen minutes for you," she announced.

"No, you didn't," said Marti, stretching to look past her.

"I didn't?"

"Listen, the most extraordinary thing happened to me," Marti went on hurriedly. "You have to help me, Terry. And don't ask any questions. I'm looking for a tall, broad-shouldered man with sandy hair. He's wearing a tannish suit—plaid, I think. Never mind about the other one."

"What other one?"

Marti gave an impatient sigh. "Terry," she said, articulating each word carefully as if for the first and last time, "I just heard someone say he's going to kill Sheikh Hikmat, period. I don't know who said it; I don't even know when he intends to pull it off. I only know that it's going to be here in the General Assembly Building, no nonsense about it, and I've got to find him. The assassin, I mean. When I find him, I want you to keep him talking until I get the guard."

"But . . ."

"Don't ask any questions. Just help me. Now you know exactly what I know, which is next to nothing, and why I won't call a guard quite yet. I'll repeat. He's tall, with broad shoulders and sandy hair, and he's wearing a tan suit. That's all you have to know." She put her hand out and touched Terry's arm. "You with me?"

Terry laughed indulgently. "Okay, let's play detective. Am I supposed to trail after you, or can I work one side of the room while you work the other?"

"You work this room. I'll come and get you if I find him first. I'm going around to the other side." Marti turned and looked through the L, where the extension to the dining room had been opened up. "I haven't seen him here, but that doesn't mean he isn't."

"If I find him first, what do I do?" asked Terry. "Wrestle him to the ground?"

"Just dazzle him," Marti said. "You know how to dazzle, don't you?"

"I haven't failed yet, chief. What then?"

"I'll come around in a couple of minutes and check you out. If I don't, then I've found him. In which case, you're off the hook."

Terry gave a characteristically lazy smile and wandered off. Marti, glancing back at her a few seconds later, found her standing with a small, rotund gentleman, her arm draped across his shoulder.

There was a time when Marti would have smiled, sighed and declared in an indulgent, motherly way, "That's my good old roommate. That's Terry. Let's face it; she's charming, beautiful, irresistible—and absolutely unreliable." But by now Terry's comings and goings, her fresh and failed love affairs, her life spilling over into Marti's, had begun to pall. Maybe it was this most recent fling with one Charlie Ray Hanson and Terry's decision to bunk in with him so quickly. Texas millionaire. Terry decided the words had all the magic ring she needed. Her bags packed with winter clothes, off she went to Charlie's place, leaving Marti alone again in that strange limbo of not knowing when her friend might come bursting back. Marti was getting to like the situation less and less.

"Hey!" Ian caught up with her and grabbed her arm. "Hold it, speedy."

"Later, Ian." She shrugged him off.

"You're going about it all wrong," he advised her, but the crowd closed around him as Marti escaped hurriedly into the next room. A line had formed in front of the buffet table at the far end of the room. She traversed its length, gazing at everyone in the line. Whoever he was, the man she was looking for wasn't hungry.

"Come stand here in my place for a second, please, Marti." The head of her subcommittee, Virginia Upson, a lanky, white-haired woman with a prominent jaw and a sharp nose, beckoned to Marti from the halfway point in the line, not expecting a refusal. "I'll be right back. I see what's-his-name over there, and I've been trying to get hold of him for a month now. They're utterly impossible when it comes to returning phone calls." She patted Marti's shoulder and went tearing off.

Marti blanched but had no choice. "Okay, but please hurry," she called. As the line snaked along, Marti carefully perused the guests, who stood around chatting, drinks in hand.

Perhaps the security wheels had already started grinding. There were never any guards at diplomatic parties, and she couldn't see any now, but one would be there soon, she supposed. He'd be wandering discreetly around, looking for the woman in red, namely, Marti Holland. That is, if he had done his duty and read her name tag correctly.

There were light suits and dark suits and, yes, plaid suits of a tan color. Most of the guests had come straight from work, but there were outsiders, too, more formally dressed. The wives of diplomats were in sequins, but there were many women in late-afternoon clothes like hers, clothes purchased, as the advertisements assured, to go directly from the office to a dinner date.

But there was no match yet of sandy hair, height, broad shoulders and tan suit, possibly plaid.

Suddenly a line of sight opened between Marti and the window opposite, which faced the East River. There he was with his stocky friend, both men with their backs to the room.

Then the line of sight closed again. Marti caught her breath. "That's the man," she said out loud.

"Pardon me?" The woman in front of her turned and smiled at Marti.

"Oh, I'm sorry. I was talking to myself," Marti said, her heart beating unnaturally fast. He was there. It was almost certainly he. She had glimpsed him only quickly, of course, and from the back, but tantalizingly, as though he were some strange creature able to appear and disappear at will. And Virginia nowhere in sight.

She had to act fast. They could be gone in a minute, but Marti was left crawling along, wringing her hands, holding Virginia's place for her. She was almost at the buffet table now. Where was Virginia? Mountains of catered food were being served, all of it with the vaguely boring, plastic look of so many of the receptions she attended in the course of her job. They really could change caterers, she thought inconsequentially. Then, at last, Marti's turn came. The waiter gave her a tiny, expectant smile. "How the devil do I know what Virginia eats?" she muttered, and removed herself from the line at once.

She surveyed the two men from across the room. They stood side by side, with drinks in their hands, their backs to the room. No one had come up to them. There was, in fact, something very private and self-contained in their very stance.

They were, to all appearances, interested in the river traffic, the view of the borough of Queens across the way, anything but the killing of Sheikh Hikmat in two weeks' time, when he came to address the General Assembly of the United Nations.

Marti made her way toward them, pausing to lift a glass of champagne from a passing tray. She had no game plan, no willpower, no nerve and absolutely no idea why she was acting on her own. But she plunged on ahead, following some impulse she made no attempt to define.

He was tall, broad shouldered and slender hipped. His well-shaped head was capped by soft, sandy-colored hair. He stood at ease, his hand encircling a squat old-fashioned glass. She guessed he was a man very much in charge; a man, she was certain, in possession of a deep, resonant voice.

She looked around for a guard and gave a start when she realized there were now several moving around the room. Searching for her, no doubt. Her red suit was a beacon, but there were other women in bright red, and the guards would have to proceed slowly and carefully. They had literally nothing to go on. Find Marti Holland, question her, and she would lead them to the villain. If she hadn't gone suddenly mad. If he existed.

It was only a matter of time. She quickened her step, brushing past several perfumed women who did not seem to want to give way. Would she speak French or English? Or would she merely drop her glass of champagne all over him and then mutter a thousand apologies?

"That your guy?" Terry came up close and whispered in her ear when Marti was no more than five yards away from her quarry.

"Maybe," she found herself saying grimly. "I can handle it from here on in."

"Hey, I don't mind. He looks awfully good from the back. Big shoulders, narrow hips. Too bad I said I'd meet Charlie Ray downstairs."

"Terry!" Marti turned imploring eyes on her friend, and Terry, surprised, gave a quick laugh.

"Okay, okay, only trying to help."

"Right." Marti turned away, embarrassed. "I'm sorry, but I'm not even certain how to handle this thing. And then I'm afraid to scare him off."

"Don't handle it yourself. Call a guard. Want me to?"

"No!" Her own sharp response made even Marti draw up short.

"This is turning into something very strange, then," Terry announced, frowning.

"If there's anything to handle, I'll handle it," Marti told her.

"Get yourself in deep enough and you'll find yourself in the center of an international *scandale*."

An international scandal. Marti gazed at the sandy-haired man. He had turned slightly to lift the glass to his lips. Marti caught a quick glimpse of his profile: straight nose, smooth brow, strong jaw. Handsome. It set her back a bit.

"Wish I had my distance glasses with me," Terry said. "He looks awfully good to me. Who do you suppose he is? Want me to reconnoiter? I'd like to see the details close up."

"Terry, he's a dangerous man."

Her friend gave an incredulous laugh. "You're sure?"

"No, I'm not sure of anything, and that's why I'm trying to play it very cool."

"You know what you're doing, Marti?"

"Absolutely not. I'm an economist, not the CIA, and I'd like to be minding my own business."

"Hey, come on, get a little action in your life. You're too tight. Unwind, unwind."

"Unwind?" Marti did not trouble to hide her impatience.

Terry gave her a long look and then seemed to come to some conclusion. "Right, you always know what you're about, and maybe that's the trouble. Anyway, I'm taking off. I promised to meet Charlie downstairs right about now. Which reminds me, I'm coming by over the weekend for the rest of my winter clothes, okay? It looks as if I'm hunkering down with Charlie at least until New Year's."

"Charlie Ray Hanson," Marti commented dryly, not taking her eyes off her quarry and wishing Terry would go away. "When am I scheduled to meet this famous lover?"

"Anytime, old roommate. He's downstairs in the lobby. You can meet him right now."

"As usual," Marti said, turning to face her friend, "it's the wrong time."

She received a long look from Terry, one that revealed the sincere compassion of which she was very capable. "We'll have dinner or something, yes? With Charlie?"

"Sure. I guess I'll be leaving, too," Marti said distractedly, "right after I handle this."

"Call me, okay? I want to hear the end of your saga."

"Right," Marti said. Then, on impulse, she added, "Oh, Terry, I'd hate anybody at the mission to know about it—until I'm ready to tell, that is."

"I definitely don't want to be involved," Terry assured her, moving quickly away.

Marti waited for a long moment, juggling her options. She decided at last on the direct approach and then went rapidly, heart pounding, over to the pair at the window before she could change her mind.

"Beautiful view, isn't it?" she said at once, in English, insinuating herself between them, willing her heart to resume its normal pace. She saw his reflection in the glass, saw herself standing there between them, the woman in red. "Nothing like the sight of river traffic to stir the juices and make you wish you were on your way somewhere else."

"Either that or to be glad you're indoors talking to a beautiful woman." His voice, of course, was just what she had expected, the voice of the man speaking French in the delegates' lounge just a little while before.

Now, however, he addressed her in English, his accent British. She turned slowly and looked him full in the face, holding on to her glass tightly, as if for support. With a sharp intake of breath, she was at once convinced that in spite of his familiar voice, he couldn't be the man she'd been chasing.

Standing before her was the most intensely masculine man she'd ever encountered. There was a certain suppressed energy about him, as though for just the moment, because of that time and place, he was keeping himself in control. He studied her with a gaze at once arrogant and curious. His eyes were of a wildly translucent blue, flashing an inner vitality she found unnerving. He was perhaps two or three years older than she, in his mid-thirties. He was deeply tanned, and there was a dimple in his right cheek. Another marked his strong chin.

She was certain he'd heard her sudden intake of breath. She was certain he was used to it. She was even certain he was smiling at her because of it.

He fixed her with his magnetic gaze and then abruptly held his hand out. "I'm Gideon Sanders, and this is David Lund. And you are?" Then he caught sight of her name tag. "Marti Holland of the U.S. Mission. How do you do, Marti Holland of the U.S. Mission."

"How do you do?" She put her hand in his and felt it grasped tightly, warmly, and held as if he weren't about to let her go. But there was something in the air, too, something that vaguely worried her. She had the feeling that somehow her turning up hadn't surprised him at all. She smiled at his companion. "Mr. Lund."

"Miss Holland." Lund took up her hand when Sanders at last released it. His accent was English, but when he bent over her hand and kissed it, his manner was old-fashioned and continental.

Lund's face was round, serious. He wore eyeglasses, but behind the soft gray of his eyes she thought she detected something kindly, some empathy reaching out. But no, she mustn't allow herself to be taken in.

"And what do you do for the U.S. Mission?" he asked.

She hesitated before answering. Suddenly she wanted her job to be glamorous and exciting, without one statistic to its name. "I'm with the economics subcommittee," she replied at last, because they were waiting and because the only glamorous alternative she could think of was secretary-general of the United Nations. "And you're with?" She let the question dangle.

"Of no mission in particular," David Lund put in almost too hastily.

"I see. Something to do with Morocco, then." One spoke French in Morocco.

"Guests of the ambassador," Gideon Sanders said, his smile unexpectedly like that of a little boy caught in a practical joke, "although we hardly know the gentleman."

"I don't suppose many people do." Marti waved her hand at the huge crowd. "These affairs are just part of protocol and afford the host country a certain amount of visibility."

Sanders continued to look interested. "Do they have these receptions often?"

"Are we discussing Moroccans or missions?"

"Take your pick. I presume you've been to more than one."

"So I have," she said. "The countries take turns giving receptions either here or at their missions, or on increasingly rare occasions, in hotels. Austerity is pretty much the name of the game these days."

"A necessary evil, though, I suppose," Sanders said.

His blue-eyed gaze was direct and extremely disconcerting. Nevertheless, Marti didn't flinch; rather, she boldly returned it. "Very necessary," she responded. "It's when people meet socially and iron out all sorts of serious problems." She couldn't help feeling that they were merely trading words, that there was some kind of testing behind it, on his part as well as hers.

"And what serious problems are you going to work out with me?" Sanders asked, a smile playing around his lips, although he continued to watch her out of thoughtful eyes.

Marti felt the heat stain her cheeks. For an extraordinary moment she had almost forgotten why she had approached them. *Damn,* she thought, *he's in control, and in a moment I'll be backing away if I'm not careful.* She reminded herself that he was the man who had threatened the life of Sheikh Hikmat. "You seem to know nothing of UN doings," she remarked, ignoring his banter in an attempt to regain her equilibrium. "What mission did you say you were with?"

"I didn't," Sanders told her.

Lund touched her arm lightly. "Miss Holland, excuse me for a moment. That buffet table is sending me signals loud and clear. Anything I can get for you?"

"No—no, thanks," she said, holding up her champagne, which she hadn't touched.

"Refresh it for you?"

"No, thanks, really."

"Gideon?"

Sanders shook his head no, his eyes on Marti. "I'm fine, thanks."

"Accounting for both of you being slender and yours truly otherwise," noted Lund before taking off.

Marti thought she detected a conspiratorial gaze passing between the two men. She wondered whether they might have seen her in the lounge, standing there, unable to move. Perhaps they had realized that their voices had carried and that she had heard them. *No,* she thought. *Impossible.* She had been as hidden as they by the huge supporting column.

But when Sanders turned back to her, it was with a look of fresh curiosity, the look of a man who had just met a woman he might be interested in and was glad of the opportunity to be alone with her. He studied her for a moment before speaking. Marti smiled at him, a cocktail-party smile. She wondered why she wanted him to be pleased with what he saw.

"Marti," he stated at last. "Your name has a decidedly un-American ring."

"My mother was deep into Hemingway when I was born. One of his characters was named Martina. I've always been grateful she wasn't partial to Russian novels."

His smile was slow in coming. She had the feeling that he stored information until it was useful to him. "But Russian diminutives are quite wonderful. Marushka—that might be one. Little Marti." He nodded his head. "I think I like Marushka."

She found herself flushing, as though by pronouncing the word he had discovered something intimate about her. The noise level in the room had risen. People milled around them, balancing glasses and forks and plates of food. He bent closer, turning his head slightly as if he wanted to hear everything she had to say.

"I can't place your accent, Mr. Sanders," she said in a rush, gripped by an unreasoning panic that he might go away if she couldn't keep him busy talking. "It's British but not quite."

He reached out with his hand still wrapped around his glass and with one finger drew her hair back behind her ear, his finger softly grazing her neck. She experienced a pale, quick shiver and wondered, in a moment of fear, whether he had noticed it.

"Yes," he said, "I get it all the time, that question about where I come from. Sometimes I think of moving to Brooklyn or someplace down South for a year. I think I'd like that—a local American dialect."

"But your accent is wonderful," she persisted, "and quite distinctive. British but not exactly." Instinctively, she reached up and fingered her earring, feeling the spot at her neck that he had touched.

He acknowledged her compliment and continued to watch her thoughtfully.

She faltered as she asked the question once more. "I'm sorry, what country are you from?"

Again the silence and at last the words, spoken with a kind of thrilling pride. "I'm Israeli, Ms Holland; Israeli born and bred. They call us Sabras."

Chapter Two

Sabra. The word seemed to freeze and hang visibly in the air between them. Suddenly everything had come full circle. Marti's fingers tightened around the champagne glass. For a fraction of a second she had let her guard slip, and believed that she was engaged in a light flirtation with an attractive stranger and that was all. One word brought her back to reality.

There were splinter groups on all sides that did not want peace in the Middle East for any number of arcane reasons. There always would be. But now, for the first time, leaders of Israel and the Arab countries were talking together, openly and with optimism. Hikmat's speech would be confirmation of a new era of trust.

"The sheikh will die here at the United Nations precisely as planned."

The words wouldn't go away. Marti had found her quarry: calmly, cleverly, just like that. She felt a rush of triumph, quickly erased when she stole a sideways glance at Sanders. Smiling, at ease and unknowable. There was no recipe for how assassins must act or be. She had heard him and could not let the matter go unreported. The words had issued clearly from Sanders's lips—in French, incongruously in French—and from no other. Sheikh Hikmat, in two weeks' time, could die at the hands of this man.

She glanced quickly around for a guard. Her view was partially blocked by a small crowd of people who were listening avidly to someone singing German lieder—Schubert, she supposed.

Sanders was speaking quietly, standing next to her and looking out over the crowd. "I acquired my British accent early on, as a matter of fact. My father was a diplomat, and we lived in England for a while when I was growing up."

Diplomat. She looked sharply at him. Complications; the house of cards in danger again. "Was a diplomat?"

"Was. Is."

"Here at the United Nations?" If his father was a member of the diplomatic community, how in the world could she accuse his son of plotting an assassination? Terry was right, of course. If she weren't careful, she'd find herself in the midst of a scandal that could destroy her career.

Gideon shook his head. "He's with the consulate in Washington."

"And you," she asked, knowing there was aggressiveness in her tone but unable to do anything about it, "aren't by any chance with the Israeli Mission? I wondered if we've met..."

His answer was slow in coming. He shook his head thoughtfully, regretfully. "I'd have remembered you if we'd met before. At any rate, I'm not with the mission. I'm a private citizen watching world democracy in action. At the moment, it appears to be well fed and very possibly on its way to getting drunk. Singing Schubert badly, I might add."

"You've a cynical cast of mind," she countered. Marti didn't know how she was managing to keep up her end of the conversation and was mildly surprised that she was. "It may well be, instead, that any number of deals, plots, counterplots and small coups are being carried out under our very noses. Schubert is just a device to confuse you."

She saw a look of quickened interest before he countered laconically, "Are we in any danger?"

Marti held his gaze. With a small missed pulse beat, she realized that he was more serious than he let on. "In any danger, right this minute? I don't suppose so. But plots," she added, watching him closely, "take more than a moment to hatch."

"You sound as if you have experience in that department."

"Oh, I?" She gave him a bright smile. "I've learned everything reading espionage novels."

"But you believe, I take it, that truth is infinitely more dangerous than fiction. Do you have any idea where we'd run and hide if this plot or counterplot suddenly gets out of hand?" He waited, smiling, putting his glass to his lips without drinking from it.

"Run and hide? I'd expect you to pull out a sword and do battle for me."

"Ah, but I'd want you somewhere safe," he said.

"Really? I've no intention of running away from danger."

"You think they'll advance on us in a frontal attack." He glanced around the room. "It's a glass box; nevertheless, it holds its secrets very close indeed. If I were plotting something, I'd want to know the hidden places in this building, the hollow walls and the air-conditioning ducts and secret closets. Danger doesn't necessarily approach with banners flying."

She held her breath. He was curious about the building, and there wasn't any doubt he was trying to find out if she could give him information. Her eye was drawn to the window. Night was complete now, and it had begun to rain; the lights across the river were misty and dim. *Dangerous waters,* she thought, both inside the building and out there in the river, which ran fast and deep and had a very strong current.

"We can always hide in my suite at the Waldorf Astoria," he said, his voice holding some amusement. "Room 1527, to be exact."

"Thanks so much. I'll try to remember that when the need arises."

"You know your way around this building, then, do you?"

"Oh, yes," she responded freely. "I worked as a guide when I was in college, and I've been plying the corridors for umpteen years since. Yes, I'd say I do."

"Anything off limits?" he asked in a casual manner.

The question elicited her first real twinge of alarm. She had been letting her guard down again, engaging in the pleasures of flirtation. "Mr. Sanders, are you trying to pick my brain?"

"Of course." His smile was charming. He put his drink to his mouth once more and downed some, regarding her over the rim with deeply serious eyes the smile hadn't reached.

"Plenty of places, then," she commented. Impulsively, she added, "When I was acting as a girl guide, my boyfriend was assistant to the chief engineer." A mote of remembrance lit her eyes. She'd been daring, testing authority, having fun. "We found all sorts of secret places that decorate the building's innards," she went on, watching closely for his response. "Have I helped you any?"

"Enough. You've told me you were a naughty little girl with the assistant chief engineer. I like your smile, by the way. One moment you're dead serious, and the next—*voilà!* the bright lights of Broadway."

She flashed him a smile, feeling the warmth suffuse her face at this compliment. The bright lights of Broadway, indeed!

He pointed to the noisy crowd that shifted and drew apart and came together again like an uncertain amoeba. "Anybody here we should be afraid of? You talked plots and counterplots."

"Strictly metaphor, Mr. Sanders," she said, still a little breathless from his compliment. "Everyone at the United Nations plays a dual role."

"You mean everyone's a spy or a rebel or an assassin, take your pick?"

Her heart tripped at his words. "No, I didn't mean that at all. Everyone here is a member of the world community and yet very much a patriot. It's not an easy combination to deal with on any level."

"Patriotic paranoia, pure and simple."

She hesitated for a moment before speaking. "Do you know a lot about paranoia, being the son of a diplomat?"

He laughed. "I know a lot about paranoia from being in the movie business."

"The movie business?" Marti stared at him in confusion. "Back up," she wanted to say. "We're going a little too fast, and in the wrong direction!"

Unexpectedly he laughed, perhaps at her surprise. He moved closer to her, spontaneously putting his hand on her arm. "You know—lights, camera, action? But we don't want to talk about it, because I'm much more interested in what's going on around here."

She felt the warmth of his body close to hers, his fingers gripping her arm for yet another moment. Then she saw two guards circling the room. It was still possible that they were looking for her. She closed her eyes against them.

While she had no doubt at all that Gideon Sanders had spoken those devastating words, once again she was paralyzed into inaction. He was the son of a diplomat, and that made all the difference. She was silently weighing her options when Sanders spoke up.

"Are you all right?"

She opened her eyes and found him regarding her worriedly. "Yes, I am—fine, I mean," she tossed off, feeling unexpectedly embarrassed. "Hard day at the office and all that."

"Perhaps you should have something to eat."

"No—no, thanks."

The guards were slowly moving in their direction, without attracting attention. Marti began to feel a tingle of panic creep along her spine. She turned toward the window, hoping the guards would miss her. She had started something and could not see her way clear to ending it. One thing was certain: if she was cornered by the guards, she would have to say it was all a mistake. She could not make a fool of herself now. She would bide her time. If Gideon Sanders had to be stopped, she would find other means to do it.

Marti slipped out of her jacket. She wore a black blouse beneath. That did it. Her name tag was gone, too, buried in the folds of the jacket.

"You're right," he said. "It is warm in here. Refill?" he asked, reaching for her glass. "No, I don't suppose that's a good idea." His eyes reflected the question as his gaze found hers.

"No," she breathed, "I don't suppose it is."

"Gideon, old bean, there you are." They were joined by a tall, bluff man with a gray mustache that drooped down at the sides, giving him the look of a forlorn bloodhound. "Got in all right, did you?" He gave Marti a quick, disarming smile.

"It was easy as one-two-three. The ambassador's a charming fellow. Thanks for your help, Alec."

"Anytime. Where's David? Where's Pilar?"

"David's on the food line as far as I can tell. As for Pilar, I thought the Moroccan mission could do without the Brazilian bombshell tonight."

Alec laughed. "Maybe you're right. Well, see you to-morrow evening at Talley's, is that it?"

A tall woman in a long satin dress tugged at his arm. "Alec, we're late."

"Right, my dear. Talley's it is, then, eh, Gideon?"

Sanders glanced at Marti. "Talley's," he called after the departing figure.

"Marti! There you are." Virginia Upson materialized out of the crowd and summarily took Marti's arm. "I thought you were holding my place in the food line."

"I was."

"For two and a half minutes."

"Three."

Virginia Upson gave her a disapproving shake of the head and then turned to Gideon Sanders. "Oh, how do you do? Excuse me for stealing Marti."

"I'm afraid I can't," he replied, smiling. Then he offered his hand. "I'm Gideon Sanders."

"Nice to meet you. Just stay put, young man, and I'll have her back to you in a nonce." She flashed him her charming, practiced smile, to which she added an extra sparkle of admiration. No one, Marti concluded, women especially, would ever take Gideon Sanders lightly.

"Come along, Marti," Virginia said. "I'll have to borrow you for a while." Without further ado, she drew Marti away with her. "I want you to meet Jacques Foliere," she said when they were out of earshot. "He's going to be your baby from now on. Incidentally, I'm starving. Why did you get off the food line? Nothing's left now but the dregs. And he's a sensational-looking man," she went on without pausing for a breath. "Those incredible eyes! They could cut you in two. Who in the world is he?"

Yes, Marti thought. *His eyes.* She'd never forget them, never. "He's Israeli," she said, "but not with the mission." "He's the man who said the Sheikh would die," she added silently.

"Sanders," Virginia mused. "I wonder if..."

Marti tugged her arm loose from Virginia's grip. "Please, Virginia, stop for a moment and listen to me."

Virginia stared down her long nose at Marti, surprise and annoyance clearly revealed on her face. "What is it?"

"Gideon Sanders over there. Virginia, I have to talk to you about him."

"Marti, not now. The last thing I need is a chronicle of your love life."

"But—"

"Come along, come along."

Marti glanced across the room through the thinning crowd. "Just a minute," she protested, but she knew it was too late. Gideon Sanders was no longer standing by the windows. In fact, he was nowhere in sight. Marti felt a stab of fear mixed inextricably with the most excruciating disappointment.

"CAN I DROP YOU somewhere—offer you a drink, perhaps?"

Marti glanced around the cavernous lobby of the General Assembly Building. It was nearly empty. The security office was one flight below, but there was no reason to explain herself to Jacques Foliere. "No, thanks. I've—uh, there's someone I have to see." Marti extended her hand, and Foliere held it for a moment in his strong grip.

"I was hoping we could spend a little more time talking informally about the project," he said wistfully. He was a tall, slender man of about her own age, with a pointed face, honey-colored hair and entirely too serious a demeanor. He said he was from the Auvergne and that he was a farmer's son, this expert on growing grains in dry climates.

"I was hoping tomorrow's lunch would be informal," she told him.

"If we expect Sheikh Hikmat to underwrite the pilot project in the Sudan," he said, "we'll have to go to him quite prepared."

Marti held her breath for just a moment. Sheikh Hikmat. The name had surfaced not fifteen minutes earlier, and from Jacques Foliere's lips. The powerful sheikh was interested in agronomy and might be just the man to back the pilot program Marti had devised. Foliere had said he was fairly certain he could wangle an appointment with him at UNESCO headquarters in Paris before the sheikh's trip to the United Nations. He'd then handed Marti a copy of the sheikh's travel schedule, remarking lightly that she might get an appointment if he could not.

"Surely you don't expect me to go along," she said, frowning.

He put his hand over hers and patted it, smiling. "We'll talk about it at lunch tomorrow, then. Good night, Miss Holland." He bent over her hand and put cool lips to it.

"Good night, Monsieur Foliere."

She stood in the lobby watching as he made his way out. Her conversation with him, like her exchange with Gideon Sanders, had lasted perhaps fifteen minutes. Yet had Gideon Sanders offered to extend the evening, she would have accepted with alacrity.

She stirred herself and began to walk across the lobby, her heels clicking on the marble floor. She would march into the security office, tell her story once and for all and disclaim further interest. Period. She'd never see Gideon Sanders again, or gaze into his blue eyes. She owed him nothing, and that was that.

"Marti—hey, Marti!"

Recognizing Terry's voice, she turned and found her roommate moving quickly toward her with a lean, elegant, gray-haired man in tow. Charles Ray Hanson, she supposed, wondering why they were still in the building at seven o'clock in the evening.

"What luck!" Terry said. "We were just talking about you. This is Charles Ray Hanson. Marti Holland." She beamed with pleasure as though showing off an expensive new bauble.

Marti found herself looking into a pair of amused, dark eyes as her hand was taken by Hanson's. The grip was strong and sure; the touch, dry and cool.

"Terry's roommate," he said softly, with a trace of a Texas accent. "Leave it to my girl to tell me everything about you except how pretty you are."

Marti cast a confused look at Terry, who merely laughed. "I'm not in the least interested in Marti's good looks. She's the smartest person I know, and that's interesting."

"Go ahead," Marti said gaily. "Discuss me as if I weren't here."

Terry and Hanson smiled at each other in an intimate, glittering way. Marti guessed that they had been drinking. Gently she extricated her hand. "How come you're still here, anyway?"

"Oh, we were in the delegates' lounge having a drink," Terry said. "I'm trying to impress Charlie with all the ambassadors I know. Where are you off to?"

"Come along and have dinner with us," Hanson offered before Marti could reply. "I know a place that serves terrific Tex-Mex food."

"Sorry," Marti said. "I've an appointment right now."

Terry tucked her arm through Hanson's. "For dinner?"

Marti shook her head. She was anxious to get away and worried that Terry might remember their conversation at the reception. The last thing she wanted to do was discuss Gideon Sanders with her roommate. "I'm beat," she said.

"Right after my appointment I'm heading home and into a hot bath without stopping to take my clothes off."

Hanson laughed. "Mind if we come around and watch?"

"Listen," Terry said, "I was just telling Charlie that I'd have to stop by the apartment for the rest of my things. I'll need some of my summer clothes, too. We've been talking about a quick trip to the Caribbean in a couple of weeks. Is this weekend okay with you?"

"Sure," Marti said. "Anytime. You're taking up space in my closet, too, Terry." This weekend she would tell Terry that she wanted the apartment to herself, period. That she was tired of Terry's possessions cluttering up the apartment. That she could afford to pick up the rent by herself. That she was fed up with Terry's euphoric goodbyes, followed days, weeks or months later by deflated hellos.

Terry disengaged herself from Hanson. Taking Marti's arm, she drew her friend aside as if she didn't want Hanson to hear her. "I'm still your roommate, Marti. I'm going to pay my share of the rent. You know, insurance?"

Marti shot a look at Hanson, who quite clearly had heard every word Terry said. *Why, he's married,* she thought, *and neither of them cares.*

"You're sure about dinner?" Hanson smiled encouragingly.

"I have to go now." Marti was aware of her peremptory tone but didn't feel inclined to apologize for it. She wanted to get away, to go about her business, to mull over this latest development in her life. Something exciting and indefinably wonderful had happened to her not half an hour before, and she didn't want to lose it, not quite yet.

"Come on," Terry was urging. "Have dinner with us. I always wanted you two to meet."

"I'll take a raincheck."

Hanson looked directly into her eyes. "It's a promise."

She went quickly toward the staircase. Charles Ray Hanson was a charmer, all right. Maybe she was wrong. Maybe he wasn't married. Maybe he was the one for Terry after all. Maybe he would be the one to free her from a life-style she no longer wanted, thereby liberating Marti, too.

THE SECRETARY to the chief of security didn't bother looking up from her work when Marti came into the office. "Go right in," she said. The door to the room beyond was open, and before Marti could make a step, a pleasant voice called from within:

"Miss Holland?"

"Yes." She went over to the door, then hesitated for a moment before stepping into the chill, windowless room. Reed Douglas, the chief of security, was sitting behind a gray metal desk. He was a big red-faced man in a well-tailored double-breasted suit. The look he gave Marti through tinted aviator glasses was openly appraising. "I figured you'd show up sooner if not later. Come in and take a load off your feet."

"I'm sorry," Marti said, taking the chair that the security chief indicated. "I didn't know you were expecting me."

"I was told you were chasing after an assassin who got away."

"I thought I was, too," Marti said. "Except now I'm wondering about it." She paused for a moment and then said, "Obviously the guards know who I am and where I was the whole time."

Douglas shrugged. "We wouldn't be doing our job if we didn't take every crank tale seriously."

"Crank tale?" Marti tried to stifle her annoyance. "Do I look like a crank?"

Douglas gave her an apologetic shrug. "I'm not sure I know what a crank is supposed to look like. I have no opinions on the subject. My men saw you at the Moroccan shindig talking casually with somebody—big, sandy-colored hair, tan suit? Wasn't that your description? They figured you'd signal them when to approach, which you didn't. Besides, one of the guards recognized him. Gideon Sanders. Then there was the other one, from the French Mission." He glanced down at a note on his desk. "Jacques Foliere."

Marti did not try to hide her surprise. "Was there anyone I talked to that you didn't check out?"

Douglas merely smiled.

"No, not Jacques Foliere," Marti said. "Wrong voice, and French is his native language."

"You're sure about those two points, then?" Douglas said. "The voice and the accent?"

"I'd better be sure about something."

"All right, why don't you begin at the beginning. I'll tell you where you've gone wrong, if you've gone wrong."

Marti recounted in detail everything that had occurred from the moment she overheard the conversation to the time Gideon Sanders had disappeared from view. When she stopped, however, it was without explaining why she had decided not to turn him in just yet. She was uncertain about her own motives in the matter. Was it because his father was in the diplomatic service, or was it that first flash of interest when he had turned his eyes on her?

Douglas thought for a while. "I'm curious about that sound—you know, the way his voice apparently bounced off the window. Where exactly did you say it happened? That's something we've never noticed before."

"Just to the right of the post near the window, the one at the entrance to the lounge. I imagine he was on the left side; I was on the right side. Somehow his voice echoed back to me."

"And you made no attempt to tell him you were there?"

"I was just about to when I heard the words that prompted me to report him."

"Well," said the security chief, "there's nothing mysterious about what Gideon Sanders said. He is a moviemaker—a director, to be exact—and what he was doing today was snooping around the place. I'm curious about how he got invited to the reception. Well, with his connections..." He raised an eyebrow at Marti, as if she might be able to tell him.

Suddenly Marti remembered the gentleman with the drooping mustache and the satin-gowned woman who had dragged him away. Alec, that was his name. He and Gideon had talked about meeting tomorrow at Talley's.

"We don't want him to make his film here," Douglas went on, "and we told him so. What he's done is to hire Hale Walker, who's an expert on security and used to be an adviser to my former chief. Hale's an expert like you're an expert."

"As a matter of fact," Marti said, "I think I know a devil of a lot about the layout of this building. I've been up and down the corridors for a long time. Besides—" But she stopped, omitting the explanation of her days as a guide and what she had learned about the guts of UN headquarters.

Douglas shook his head. "Sanders wants to know about things like air ducts. I said nothing doing. He's going to have to wing it. Authentic he's not going to get, not even from Hale Walker."

"What kind of movie?" Marti asked.

"They're calling it *Checkpoint*," Douglas told her. "They gave me a summary of the script. It has to do with an assassination attempt on the life of a sheikh. There's your mysterious remark. It's just coincidence that Sheikh Hikmat is going to speak two weeks from now."

"Coincidence." Marti closed her eyes briefly. Suddenly she was very tired and hungry, and Douglas's face was unexpectedly taking on the aspect of a small, unfriendly dog.

"Not a coincidence exactly," he went on. "Plenty of Middle Eastern potentates pass through town. Sooner or later they get to address the General Assembly." The telephone rang. Douglas turned and picked it up, nodding at Marti to wait. "Yeah, right; yeah, right," he said into the receiver. "I'll get on it. Right." He hung up, clearly prepared to dismiss Marti.

"We'll keep an eye on Sanders if he shows up again," he told her. "We don't want him trying any smart tricks, either, just to make his movie. The trouble is, his father's with the Israeli Embassy in Washington. He knows everybody, so I don't suppose we've seen the last of him. But we get and turn down all kinds of requests to use the building, especially during the General Assembly, so we're not new at the game of refusal. Since the General Assembly runs for only three months out of the year, the rest of the time we can relax the rules a little bit. But not now; definitely not now. Your friend Sanders tried to pull a few strings, but no way. We've had string pullers before."

"But if in fact he was planning something—an assassination, I mean—the movie would be a perfect cover-up," Marti pointed out.

"So would just about anything else you can name," Douglas remarked dryly.

Marti stood up. "Okay, just doing my duty. It's a load off my mind. I'm going to go home now and forget all about it."

"Well," Douglas told her magnanimously, "you did the right thing by coming to us. We have plenty of problems. Diplomatic immunity leaves large holes in our ability to police, let me tell you." He got heavily to his feet and moved past her to the door. "We have just so much power and no more." He put his hand out, and Marti shook it without enthusiasm.

"No, I'm not going to give it one more thought," Marti said, but she knew it wasn't true. Even though it was now confirmed that Gideon was a harmless movie director, she didn't want to trust him fully. The Israelis, the Russians, even the Americans—everyone could, or need not, play dual roles, but there was no counting him out. Coincidence, maybe—and then again, maybe not.

"You'll have to show me exactly where that acoustical oddity is," Douglas added as Marti moved toward the outer door.

"Anytime," she said. "I'm with the economic subcommittee, Virginia Upson's group."

"Right. I know all about you. I'll give you a call tomorrow."

After Marti had closed the door behind her, she stood quietly for a moment, feeling wrung out. They knew all about her. The thought somehow was chilling.

Outside the building, Marti hugged her raincoat close and looked up at the sky. All that was left of the grim, rainy evening was a halo of muddied light reflected in a pool of water near the bus stop. Back there, in the building, the party would be coming to an end around now. For a while, something had happened to her, some spark that had set her into action. It was sputtering now. Soon it would be gone, and she would be the same safe-and-sound Marti Holland. She caught sight of her bus heading up the avenue. Home. If only she had had the nerve to tell Terry to let go once and for all.

Chapter Three

David Lund stood near the window of his Manhattan suite, which overlooked the UN complex on the opposite side of the avenue.

He jingled some coins in his pocket, all the while staring with undisguised curiosity across the room at Gideon Sanders. "Assassin? Marti Holland!"

"It fleetingly crossed my mind," Gideon said.

"Wait a minute. Are we talking about that Marti Holland? The green-eyed babe who moved in on us just about an hour ago, that Marti Holland? You've been reading one script too many, my friend. Assassins may come enticingly packaged, but they don't blow their cover quite so obviously."

"I believe that truth is stranger than fiction. I'm a film director, remember?"

"So you are, Gideon, so you are."

Gideon Sanders crossed his long legs and settled back in the deep-cushioned chair, the most comfortable one in Lund's apartment. He had both hands cupped around a short-stemmed glass, warming the amber cognac within. "And if I were buying the script on this one, maybe that's just what I'd ask for: the truth that's stranger than fiction." He took an appreciative sip of the cognac, letting its soft fire course down his throat.

He squinted at a watercolor on the opposite wall without really taking in its content.

"This is the scenario the way I see it, Dave." He put the glass down and framed a square with his fingers. "Scene one: the United Nations; a big, glamorous reception given by the head of the Moroccan Mission. Glamorous," he added after a moment's pause, "but sedate. At the party are two men representing two countries, Israel and Great Britain. To all eyes they are either diplomats or businessmen having a quiet drink, discussing diplomacy or business, whatever the case may be. Their mission, however, is a delicate one."

"To put it mildly," David threw in.

Gideon ignored him. "The Israeli is in reality the businessman he appears to be. He has another mission in life, however, as a member of the Israeli Secret Service. The chap from Great Britain is in Her Majesty's Service in precisely the same capacity. On the surface, he appears to be an executive with an international conglomerate. *Sub-rosa*, he's committed, as is the Israeli, to the good fight. That is, wherever danger appears that might harm the peace process to which their countries are committed, one might find men like these. Quiet, fitting into the community and deadly serious. The two men are not discussing business; rather, they are discussing a message received from Israel."

David smiled around the pipe he was trying unsuccessfully to light. "I think I've heard this story before, but go on."

"They've received news about an assassin, a cool killer from abroad who's been hired to pull down a certain sheikh during his peace-loving mission to the United Nations. The reason? Kill the sheikh and make it look as if the Israelis are the villains. The object of our two gentlemen? Search and destroy the assassin before he can act."

"She," David put in. "According to your scenario."

Gideon grinned. "Right."

Lund nodded. Impatiently, he threw down the unlit pipe and then crossed the room to the liquor cabinet. After hesitating for a moment, he poured himself a club soda with a generous splash of scotch. "Great scenario, Gideon, considering it matches perfectly with everything that's happening, both in the film and in reality."

"In the film," Gideon reminded him in a dead-serious tone, "the villain is caught."

"And a few other people die in the bargain."

They were both quiet for a while, studying the possibilities. David examined the crystal glass in his hand. He held it up to the light and watched the play of color. As the New York representative for a Geneva-based bank, Intertrust, one of Lund's perks was to live, rent free, in the corporation's apartment, but he never felt quite comfortable in its huge, cold rooms. "What worries me more than the Marti Hollands of the world," he said at last, "is reality overlapping the movie."

"Ah," said Gideon, "but here's where this script differs from *Checkpoint*. Our assassin is a beautiful green-eyed lass who comes into the reception with one purpose in mind: to find the men with the mission and put them out of action. Phase number one in her planned pursuit of the head of state."

"What makes you think Marti Holland fits the bill? It's true I'm a little wary of women who sneak up unannounced, beautiful or not. In fact, the more beautiful, the less I trust."

Gideon stood up and restlessly began to roam the length of the room. Green eyes, brown hair and a sprinkling of freckles across the bridge of her nose. He had longed to bend down and plant a kiss across that pale sprinkling. "She came into the reception," he recounted, "and looked carefully around as if for someone. A tall, horse-faced creature came up to her, but our heroine—''

''Heroine!'' David interjected with a laugh.

''Heroine,'' Gideon emphasized. ''Green-eyed women are always heroines, even when they're assassins. Even with freckles. But to go on with the plot. Our heroine didn't seem too pleased to meet up with this horse-faced creature—at least that's the impression I received. They talked for a moment. Marti Holland then went and stood on the food line. Her eyes played the crowd.''

''You saw all this,'' David said, looking at him with increased respect, ''while talking to me about the problems of crashing the UN building and digging out its innermost structural secrets.''

Gideon stopped, his brow creased. ''There are women who possess a kind of inner power, one they're almost unaware of. Our assassin has that power. Certainly not a great beauty, but she came into the room alight with purpose.''

''And you've worked out the purpose,'' Lund commented dryly.

Gideon laughed once again. ''I'm busily script writing. We were facing the room when she came in. Then, when we turned around, I caught her reflection in the window. At first I had to do a little sifting to match her hair and red suit.''

''All this while we were discussing ways and means of breaking into the building late at night.''

''All this.''

''I can say one thing for you, Gideon: it's obvious you can jump rope and chew gum at the same time. Is that what the Americans say?''

Gideon ignored the remark, his mind reconstructing Marti's progress at the reception. ''When she got to the head of the food line, she suddenly turned and walked away empty-handed. She was headed quickly, determinedly, in our direction when someone interrupted her—a tall, glamorous brunette, incidentally. They looked in our direction for a bit, but Marti disposed of this someone quickly. Oh, and to fortify herself, she picked up a glass of champagne, but I doubt she ever took a sip of it. Without further ado, she made a beeline for us. Although…" He didn't finish the sentence, because he couldn't quite believe it, either. There had been something a little raw and diverting about the way she had moved in on them. Smooth words, yes—she was a practiced diplomat—but still…something. And he didn't want to discuss it with David, not at the moment.

"I'm afraid I'm not quite convinced," David said after a while. "The lady merely did what aggressive American women do under such conditions. She saw two men—unattached for the moment—and moved in. I wouldn't attach any more significance to it than that."

"Sell me on it, then," Gideon challenged him. "Her innocence, I mean." He went over to the window, looked down onto the avenue and then came quickly away. Throwing himself down on the couch, he grabbed his drink and finished it in a gulp. He was getting antsy. He didn't like hanging around doing nothing more than chewing over possibilities when somewhere in the city there might be a very special killer on the loose.

"Aha!" Lund poked a finger in his direction. "Out of the blue arrives a young woman with an extraordinary knowledge—so you say—of the physical workings of that plant across the way. How very convenient of her to have told you all that. What she really wants is a part in your movie, and there isn't anything she won't do to make certain she gets it." Then he added after a long pause during which neither man moved, "There are all sorts of variations on that script, Gideon, including the simple one of pitching the movie director, period."

Gideon was a long time answering. Lund had been in the business too long. There had been a look in Marti Holland's eyes: curiosity, distrust, something a little hard and distant—and yet she had held tenaciously on until the officious horse-faced woman hauled her away.

Lund picked up the bottle of cognac and refilled Gideon's glass. Then he sat down opposite him in a club chair, putting his feet up on a matching hassock. "Gideon, men like you should have wives waiting for them back home just so you'll stay out of trouble."

Gideon smiled and sipped the cognac. "I almost made that mistake once. The first thing she wanted to do was travel along with me."

"You couldn't have cared very much about her, then, if that was the reason to break it up."

Gideon swirled the cognac slowly in the glass. It was true, of course. He'd had a bee in his bonnet at the time. He had sat for a while in the Israeli parliament, all wild oats having been carefully sown in the Negev Desert during those earlier years of army life. Maybe it had something to do with hitting the grand old age of thirty. Two years later the restlessness had come again, the wanting to move, to accomplish something on a broader scale.

Work in the Israeli Secret Police merged with the one talent he'd always had, filmmaking. He moved from amateur to professional in the one, bringing the other along with him like a second skin.

"It's a chess game we're at," David said, returning the conversation to its original topic, "not a script for a movie. The enemy is largely unknown, however, and he hardly ever mails in his moves. It's a game we've played before on occasion, Gideon, as you well know. And you have to protect your rear while thinking far ahead. The enemy's object is to upset the chessboard and the hell with the game. Incidentally," Lund added, "I'll give you this much. After you left,

I saw your sunny little friend talking rather animatedly with Jacques Foliere."

Gideon was surprised to hear Foliere's name mentioned, but he surprised himself more with his sudden defense of Marti Holland. "She's with the United Nations. It's her job to see and be seen. She talks to everybody. She even talked to you. What's Foliere doing in New York?"

"She left the reception in his company," Lund told him in a flat voice, ignoring the question.

Gideon had to fight back a feeling of annoyance, as though somehow he had already made a claim on the assassin, on Marti Holland. He was thinking of Jacques Foliere, too, and the last time they had met. Gideon had been in Morocco about a year before during some filming at its lone studio. Foliere had stopped by with an old friend of Gideon's. He was living in Morocco at the time, working for UNESCO. They'd had lunch together, but it was a desultory affair. Each clearly had a lot to say to the other about conditions in Africa and in Europe, but they had discussed filmmaking instead.

"Maybe it's time I renewed our acquaintance," Gideon said. "It's odd that Foliere should turn up here at this particular time."

"Not so odd. He works for UNESCO. Maybe he's the man who can pull the strings for us," Lund suggested, brightening. "At any rate, I did a little quick research while I was about it. He has an apartment in the East Fifties."

"I'll ask him to the Waldorf for a drink," Gideon said. "Tonight." As he moved to get up, the telephone went off.

Lund reached for the receiver with a gesture of apology. "Lund here." He smiled, his eyes on Gideon. "Don't get excited. He's here and I'm here, and that's all." He handed the receiver over, pursing his mouth and rolling his eyes in a way that told Gideon his caller was Pilar do Valles. She was both the producer of and the female lead in *Checkpoint*.

"Pilar," Gideon said at once, watching Lund trying to hide his amusement.

"Don't 'Pilar' me," said the voice at the other end, in the husky, rapid-fire way she spoke colloquial English. "I've been waiting for you since, since—whatever. I thought we'd be having dinner together. You're working for me, remember?"

Gideon pushed his cuff back and consulted his watch. "There's no possible way I could forget, and we are, my dear, having dinner. Say about eight?"

"At Regine's, then. I'm starved. Try not to come wearing your blue denims, Gideon. A tuxedo would please me greatly."

Gideon looked down at the business suit he had put on for the Moroccan occasion. "I'll try my best, love."

"No, you won't. Gideon, are you listening to me?"

"At Regine's," Gideon repeated. "At eight. David will be along, too."

"Like hell he will. I don't like that, Gideon. I don't like that one bit. Do you expect me to attack you? Do you need a baby-sitter?"

"David wants to see you," Gideon said in a mollifying tone. "You know he's in love with you."

Lund guffawed and stretched the length of the couch, raising his arms behind his head and closing his eyes.

"Tell me about it," Pilar said, and hung up.

"What's her problem?" Lund asked lazily, clearly not expecting an answer.

"What difference does it make," Gideon said. "I just want you along. She's Intertrust's bankable movie star. I believe you should keep a weather eye on your investment."

"There are plenty of others, including her own husband, who can keep an eye on her," David noted dryly.

Two years previously, the Brazilian-born actress had appeared in a movie made in São Paolo that won several prestigious film awards. Prior to returning to Brazil and sudden celebrity status, she had spent several years in Hollywood, pursuing an unsuccessful career. Now all was changed, and she was what the movie business termed "bankable."

Married to one of the principals of Intertrust, an international banking corporation, the star had found it easy to obtain all the financing she needed to put together the production of *Checkpoint*. David Lund, like Pilar's husband, was an officer of Intertrust, although in his position he played a second, dangerous game with men like Gideon Sanders.

Gideon, who had made several successful small-budget films in Europe and Israel, had been hired to direct Pilar's production. He did not consider a liaison with his temperamental star part of the contract he had signed. He'd made it a policy never to become involved with the women he directed, not even in less exotic terrain than New York.

He thought of Marti Holland and the way she had moved in on them. His first impression had been one of amusement. She probably recognized him from the article that had appeared in Sunday's *Times*. Gideon was always in the market for nuances, but he discarded that notion almost at once. It was wrong, and he couldn't quite say why exactly.

Nothing David had said convinced him differently.

Still, he'd been genuinely sorry when the Upson woman dragged Marti away. She hadn't looked back, which also surprised him.

"We'll get a spot on her background," he told David at last, "if that'll make you happy."

"Pilar?"

"Marti Holland," Gideon said with a show of impatience, adding, "for any number of reasons. She works for the U.S. Mission, and I'm heartily sick of Walker's stupidity. I can learn more about the design of the building from our charming Miss Holland than I have in the last five weeks from the ex-security adviser to the United Nations, Hale Walker."

Lund sat up and ran a hand through his thinning hair. "An assassin who works for the U.S. Mission and will gladly impart information about the stomach rumblings of that building across the way." He grinned. "Oh, I like that, Gideon. It'll play in Peoria; it'll really play in Peoria."

He got to his feet, went over to the window and peered down into the street, five stories below. "Damn them." Lund nodded toward the UN building. Intertrust had agreed to bankroll Pilar's *Checkpoint* with the assurance that the UN would cooperate in the filming. Time was passing. When it came to a return on investment, not even do Valles's wife had unlimited access to their checkbook.

The UN public relations office had agreed to cooperate to a point and had handed them Walker, retired security chief.

Gideon joined him at the window. "We'll bust it, that glass bastion. I haven't even begun yet."

"Careful," Lund said.

The sky was the deep gray of a New York night, but with the backlighting of a city bathing in its own glow, an early-evening color that Gideon found very attractive.

"See her?" Lund asked.

"What are you talking about?"

"That woman down there in the Burberry raincoat? At the bus stop? Touch of red at her collar? I'd swear that's our green-eyed lass."

Gideon felt an unexpected, almost physical jolt at the notion. "You've got hawk eyes, my pal."

Lund picked up a pair of field glasses from a table near the window. "When she left the delegates' dining room with Foliere, I had my eyes on her. Her walk is easy, natural, self-assured. Couldn't miss it." He handed the glasses to Gideon. "What do you intend to do about her?"

Gideon put the glasses to his eyes and adjusted the focus. It was Marti Holland, all right, bundled against the late-October cold. "Handle her," he said.

"Charming young woman," David remarked. "What a shame if she's up to something."

MARTI PAUSED for a moment before pressing the light switch in the small foyer of her fourth-floor apartment. She took in the normal sounds of distant traffic and, through the wall, the reassuring murmurs from the neighboring apartment. She switched on the light. A quick glance around revealed nothing out of order. Marti had no idea what else she might have expected.

Home: four small rooms with hardly any view at all. Home, with its comfortable furniture, fireplace, kilim carpet in the living room and abstract paintings on the walls. She kicked her shoes off as she went from the foyer into the kitchen. Everything was just as she had left it. The morning dishes were still in the sink, and she had neglected to put the milk back into the refrigerator.

Normal. Everything miraculously normal. What had she expected, and why? All the way home she had sensed something about to happen, some bombshell to be dropped, something that would add a little extraordinary glamour to her life. But the trip on the bus had been as uneventful as it was every night.

She took off her raincoat and hung it up. Then she returned to the kitchen for a half-finished apricot yogurt, which she ate leaning against the sink, staring sleepily at the blue-flowered wallpaper. Blue. Cornflower? Lapis lazuli? The color of Gideon Sanders's eyes.

Oh, she thought angrily, she couldn't, she wouldn't, let herself fall so easily—and over a pair of wonderful eyes! She'd kept her emotions carefully in check these last two years, and not until now had she regretted it.

Paris and Pierre Duvall. Funny, but once she had hit the States, it had been easy enough to forget him. Not so her vulnerability. It was what made her cautious, what made her think twice, three times, ten times, about Gideon Sanders. Pierre Duvall. She could credit him with that much: the word "caution" emblazoned on her heart.

It had been her first overseas assignment, and she had considered herself blessed with good fortune. She worked for UNESCO in the world's most glamorous city. She shared a sunny apartment in Montparnasse with Emily Holden, who worked at the U.S. Embassy. She loved her work. Her life was exciting. She glided from day to day on an extraordinary high composed of a feeling of accomplishment and the very fact of Paris.

She met Pierre Duvall in the most ordinary way. She hadn't even been looking for one particular romance—romance was all around her.

She had rushed out of a meeting one day carrying a portfolio of papers in her arms. Bumping headlong into a handsome stranger, she dropped the portfolio and then stared nonplussed at the scattering of documents that lay around her feet.

He scooped them up and tucked them back into her portfolio. Then he smiled and insisted on taking her for an aperitif by way of apology.

Pierre was a diplomat who had recently returned from an assignment in Japan. In the nights that followed, she gave no thought to the future. He revealed a Paris to her that she might never have known. It was a Paris of bistros and quiet winding streets that led to the Seine. A Paris of artists in Montmartre studios and playwrights whose works were performed in tiny spaces at the end of unknown lanes. She fell in love quickly, passionately and completely. Then, after two months of happiness, it was over. The note, written on a sheet of white linen stock, was delivered to her door one morning, along with a spray of yellow roses. She had opened the note happily enough. It took a while for the contents to sink in.

"*Ma chère petite*, I've good news. The assignment in New Delhi has come through. You know how eagerly I've waited for it."

No, she hadn't known. Perhaps he had told her and she had preferred not to hear.

"It was fun, and I know our paths will cross again. Enjoy our Paris. All my love, Pierre."

"Love, Pierre." That was all. It was over, and Paris lost its charm. Marti met Virginia Upson at an embassy party, and within a few months she was back home working for the U.S. Mission to the United Nations. She had left Paris without a backward glance.

Finding an apartment in New York hadn't been easy. The location of her apartment was good, but the rent was high. She was pleased when Terry offered to share it with her. Terry, to whom life was a lark. It turned out that Marti's old college roommate would be gone more often than not, as in the old days at school. A recent pay raise and the interest from a small inheritance would now allow Marti to keep up with the rent by herself.

What a day, she thought, putting water on to boil for instant coffee. She found a piece of dry cake in the refrigerator and put it on a plate.

She went into the bedroom and stripped, listening with half an ear for the kettle to whistle. She put on a blue plaid dressing gown and made her way back into the kitchen.

Then, with the coffee and cake in hand, she went into the living room. She flopped down on the couch with the notes for her speech.

There was no concentrating on them, however. Marti was too keyed up from the events of the day.

For a little while she had flung herself into an adventure. Perhaps it had been merely one of her own making, but her senses had come alive. She had deliberately dumped it all on Reed Douglas's desk, and there was no more worrying about it.

Now her life was back to normal. The adventure had never been; Gideon Sanders was a memory.

She was home, and there was a paper to read tomorrow that offered suggestions for improving farming methods in Third World countries. Jacques Foliere would be at the meeting to offer fresh insights into the newer, hardier strains of wheat and sorghum.

The program she had devised needed funding, and while there were any number of reasons why Sheikh Hikmat should stay alive, Jacques Foliere had just suggested a new one. The sheikh was particularly interested in agronomics, and Foliere was certain he could be approached with a plan for funding a pilot program in the Sudan.

Try as she might, Marti couldn't concentrate on the matter at hand. Intense, curious blue eyes had turned upon her. She had, for a little while, basked in their light. Gideon Sanders, the Sabra who had disappeared as if he had never been.

"MARTI, CAN YOU explain it, this flirtation I seem to have with disaster? Why does everything have to happen to me?"

Marti, who had come to work early, glanced quickly at her watch. It was nine in the morning, and Virginia Upson was planted squarely in front of her desk, waving a copy of the *New York Times* in the air.

"What's wrong?"

"Jacques Foliere is what's wrong. Imagine that happening to him today of all days." Wearing an almost triumphant air of having been the first to bring her the bad news, Virginia stopped long enough to watch Marti's confused reaction.

"It's obvious you haven't cracked open the morning newspaper," she added in an unforgiving tone.

"The bus was unbearably crowded. I never even gave it a glance." Marti, her brow furrowed, reached across and took up Virginia's copy. "What happened to Jacques Foliere?"

"First page, there," said Virginia, pointing a bony finger at the two-column headline and reading it for her upside down. "'United Nations Diplomat Plunges to Death.' Jacques Foliere."

"What!" Marti cried, aware that her voice had risen an octave.

"No reasons why; suicide suspected," Virginia went on. "Now, why would that handsome, debonair man want to commit suicide? He looked perfectly happy to me."

Marti glanced at the photograph accompanying the news story. Jacques Foliere, with sandy hair, blond eyebrows, light eyes and a carefully neutral expression.

"The Waldorf-Astoria," Virginia told her. "Very lovely for the U.S. ambassador to look out of his tower window and find a body hurtling past."

"The Waldorf-Astoria?" Marti repeated, stumbling over the words. That was where Gideon Sanders was staying. "You're sure?" She quickly began to peruse the article.

"Why do I have to say everything twice?" Virginia queried with annoyance.

The story gave the time of Foliere's death as well as some vague speculation about the possibilities of suicide. There was some biographical information about the diplomat, and that was all. Marti read it carefully, aware of a faint sense of foreboding, although she could not have explained why. All the while, Virginia, her hands splayed on Marti's desk, leaned across it, explaining her predicament in a complaining tone.

"The luncheon meeting has been canceled, of course, pending their getting someone else to fill his shoes. Six months' work to hell and gone."

"The fact that Jacques Foliere is dead is just a slight inconvenience, is that all?" Marti asked, folding the newspaper in a very precise manner and handing it back to Virginia. "I mean, in the vast economic scheme of things?"

"That's as good a way to put it as any." Virginia snapped the paper under her arm and walked away, but at the door to Marti's office, she turned back. "The police will be on to you, Marti. Didn't you leave with him last night?"

Marti stared across the small office in horror. "No," she said quickly. The scene came back to her. Virginia had introduced her to Foliere. She had talked to him distractedly at the reception for all of ten or fifteen minutes, keeping her eye out for Gideon Sanders. David Lund waved to her from the opposite end of the room, but he was talking to someone, not Sanders. Marti's original plan was to stay at the reception for no more than half an hour. She felt, although her watch told her differently, as though she had been there for many hours. Then there was the chief of security. She planned to stop off and see him.

Foliere had left the delegates' dining room at the same time as Marti. He stepped into the elevator with her, chatting amiably all the way down. In the lobby, she confirmed their luncheon date, shook hands and thought no more about him.

Why, she wondered now, did she feel he had suddenly taken on significance in her life?

"We can't afford *scandales*," Virginia told her, echoing Terry's remark of the previous evening.

"Virginia, I don't know the man. The last I saw of him was when I..." She stopped, glad to see that Virginia wasn't interested in what she had to say. There was no way to bring Gideon Sanders and Reed Douglas into it, no way at all.

"Okay, then you've nothing to worry about," Virginia said in a tone that made Marti begin to worry. "Pick me up at about twenty to," she added, closing the door behind her.

Marti shook her head. "Virginia." The word slipped out as an admonition. She thought seriously about getting herself a cup of coffee to clear away the cobwebs that were draped across her brain. Instead, she turned back to her speech for that morning's conference. Something was bothering her, however, as it had ever since she'd overheard those words the day before. "The sheikh will die precisely as planned." She couldn't get rid of the feeling that she was Alice and that she had dropped down the rabbit's hole. Only this wonderland was full of pitfalls and danger, without a laugh in it.

The meeting was scheduled for ten o'clock. At precisely nine-thirty, Marti began to gather up her papers. It took a few minutes to run a brush through her hair and check her makeup. The walk from the U.S. Mission across the avenue and up to the council chambers in the General Assembly Building would take ten minutes. That included time for dodging traffic, waiting for the elevator and perhaps running into other delegates along the way. That left fifteen minutes in the chambers for a brief conference with the rest of the staff.

Her telephone went off five minutes before she had to pick up Virginia. Marti was tempted to let it ring, but in a moment of weakness she reached for it.

"Guy won't give his name," the receptionist said at once. "He's on five-oh-five. Wants to talk to you personally; said he's a friend."

"A friend." Marti did not know why Sanders's name surfaced in her mind, but it did. Then again, it had been there all along, a singular buzz that had allowed her little sleep.

"He has a nice voice," the receptionist offered helpfully.

"Ask who he is. Oh, never mind," Marti said, and punched into the call.

"Yes?" She asked the question with a touch of apprehension that was new to her. There was no reason at all why Sanders would try to find her.

The voice at the other end was low and muted, as though he were facing away from the receiver, but she knew instantly that it wasn't Gideon Sanders.

"Marti Holland?"

"May I help you?"

There was a slight pause, and then, "You have already."

"I'm sorry," she said. "I don't understand you. Could you speak a little louder?"

"We're eternally grateful to you, Miss Holland."

She discerned an accent but could not quite place it. "Really?" She waited, aware of an ominous undertone to the faint, pleasantly conversational voice of her caller. Another crank call, she decided, one she would have to dispatch with firmness.

"You did us an enormous favor, and frankly we'd like to do one for you sometime."

"If you wouldn't mind explaining yourself..." she began. "But I'm in a tremendous hurry. Could I call you back?"

"But of course we've done you a favor when you get down to it," the voice went slowly, suavely, on. "You're still alive. I'd say that's the biggest favor of all. Don't make us change our minds, Miss Holland. That was a long way down from the fifteenth floor."

"Are you talking about Jacques Foliere?"

"Would I do a thing like that? Play it safe. We don't know how you know or even what you know. We scratched an itch, that's all."

"Are you threatening me in some way?"

He laughed, and then there was a click. Marti, left holding the receiver, stared at it, her heart racing. *A crank call,* she told herself. *That's all it was.* She would have to notify Reed Douglas about it.

"Marti, get a move on." Virginia, peering in the door, beckoned to her. "I thought you lived by the clock."

"Right with you." She needed time to think and wanted nothing more to do than throw her glass paperweight at Virginia, who was frowning at her. Marti wondered crazily how she might get through the day. "Virginia," she began, "I just..."

"I have no patience for anything but the problem at hand," Virginia interrupted. "The whole world's falling in on me."

Marti got automatically to her feet, gathered her bag and her papers and was just about to follow Virginia out when her telephone rang once again. She reached out but did not pick up the receiver at once, looking entreatingly across the room at her chief.

"Oh, pick it up," Virginia said. "It'll kill you if you don't. What the devil's gotten into you?"

Marti felt a faint prickling down her spine, but since Virginia was staring so expectantly at her, she reached for the receiver. "Hello?" She was surprised at how small her voice sounded.

"Gideon Sanders," said the receptionist, "on five-oh-five. Isn't that the—"

Marti punched into the call, casting a glance at Virginia. "I'll make it brief," she said, suddenly feeling blank, as though she knew nothing, expected nothing and would understand nothing. She took a deep breath. "Marti Holland." Virginia walked away, leaving the office door open, her footsteps clicking rapidly down the corridor.

"Marti, Gideon Sanders here. I'm convinced we have a date for tonight at Talley's. Ten o'clock, is it?"

She felt a mixture of relief and fear that was so intense she had to cling to the edge of her desk for support. "Date?"

"An assignation, if you like that better. I'll pick you up at—"

"Just a minute..." Marti said. Then she stopped. Events were crowding in around her, and she wasn't being given a moment to work her way through them. They didn't have a date. There was no mistaking it, and Sanders knew it; she could hear it in his quick, charming manner. He was a man used to having his way, but she thought this time it was something else, something to do with the unthinkable. "No," she said at last, very slowly and with genuine regret, "we don't have a date, so I doubt if it could be at ten o'clock."

"Nonsense," he told her, the laughter ringing in his voice. "What did you say your address was? I'll pick you up, say, at nine. We can have a drink first."

She glanced frantically around her office as though she might somehow find a frame of reference that would bring her to her senses. All she saw was the orderly room of someone who took no chances. Philodendrons and books and at least two calendars. Clock, plus a photograph of a blond four-year-old nephew, the sort of nephew single women always had. Other people lived lives of unquiet excitement, but not Marti. Not five minutes before, someone had called her and told her he was responsible for killing Jacques Foliere. And then he had threatened her. And she had done nothing about it.

Virginia's voice calling her echoed down the corridor.

"Ten o'clock," she found herself saying to him. "At Talley's."

"See you, love."

Marti thought she had detected a note of satisfaction in his voice just before he hung up. Love? What was she to make of that?

She slammed down the receiver and ran after Virginia, full of apologies. "It's just one of those days," she said, keeping it all to herself: the telephone threat, the warmth suffusing her, the vague fear she had first felt at hearing Gideon's voice, the sudden desperate desire to go with the flow—regardless of the consequences.

Virginia was still chattering petulantly. "This isn't the end. It's always a ticklish situation when a foreign national dies under suspicious circumstances. How did Jacques Foliere strike you?"

"Pleasant enough," said Marti, hurrying to keep up with her, forcing her mind back. "We discussed today's meeting and the funding for our pilot project. He claimed he had a splendid connection with Sheikh Hikmat and said our money worries were over. Then I decided to leave, so we took the elevator down together. We said goodbye. I smiled; he smiled. I went one way; he went the other. Whether he was happy or depressed, Virginia, I'm afraid I can't tell you. Anyway, it has nothing to do with us," she went on hastily, feeling that she had spoken too fast and in too apologetic a manner, as though she were somehow the accused.

"No, I suppose not," Virginia said, her mood suddenly lifting. "All I care about now is that your paper is ready and that we'll get some action around here."

"Virginia," Marti began hesitantly, "I just got the most peculiar phone call."

"Come along, Marti; we all get peculiar phone calls."

It was only later, after four o'clock, when the conference adjourned, that the sense of foreboding that had dogged Marti all day caught up with her. She packed her papers and ran out of the conference room while Virginia was busy chatting with the delegate from Zambia. She caught a cab uptown and fifteen minutes later was locked safely in her apartment with the late edition of the paper.

FRENCH DIPLOMAT PLUNGES TO DEATH
by Rachel Boyd

New York, October 27—Jacques Foliere of UNESCO died early this morning as a result of a fall from the fifteenth floor of the Waldorf-Astoria Hotel. A police spokesman said it has not yet been determined whether Foliere jumped or fell from an open corridor window on the north side of the building—nor do they rule out foul play. There were no witnesses, and a suicide note has not been found. The police have no information as to why Foliere was in the hotel at that hour.

Foliere, 32, whose current address was 362 East 54th Street, resided in Paris, where he worked as an agricultural adviser to UNESCO. He was an expert on farm economics, particularly on farming methods in the African subcontinent. Before his current assignment, he had worked in Africa on drought-related problems. No one at the United Nations was able to provide any reason for Foliere's apparent suicide.

Marti tossed the paper aside without finishing the article. How he was found and all the other details would only add to her feeling of disquiet. She paced her living room for a while, trying to convince herself that Foliere's death had nothing to do with her apart from setting back the timetable on the economic commission's report. And perhaps ruining their chances for getting money from Sheikh Hikmat. But then, but then—maybe the sheikh would die as planned.

There was one other thing she couldn't get out of her mind: Room 1527 at the Waldorf-Astoria. Gideon Sanders's suite. On the fifteenth floor. He had told her where he was staying quite openly, almost too openly.

She was being drawn into it, whatever it was, and she was all alone. She went over to the telephone and picked up the receiver. Surely she could get to Virginia now and discuss it with her. Or Terry. Terry might help by merely listening. Then she dropped the receiver as if it had scorched her hand. Someone with a soft, insinuating voice had threatened her life. Her mysterious caller had warned her. She must not talk about Jacques Foliere's death to anyone.

Chapter Four

The evening turned out to be unexpectedly mild, as is often the case in the East after the first frost of late autumn. Marti walked over to Talley's from her apartment enjoying the balmy freshness of the air and the subtle bite of winter it held.

The restaurant, on a side street was, for all its popularity, unprepossessing. Marti came up to it slowly. Yellow light spilled out onto the dark street as if to entice passersby to sample the wares within. She stopped for a moment to peer in the window. A pure white linen curtain covered the lower half; the upper window permitted her a partial view through some leafy palms of the restaurant beyond.

A row of huge yellow globes, suspended from the ceiling, reached to the back of the restaurant. They suffused the smiling, chatting patrons with a warm, attractive glow.

Then she saw Gideon, taller than most. He was wearing a black turtleneck sweat and a tweed jacket. He moved up to the crowded bar at the front of the restaurant. There he touched someone on the shoulder, a man who turned and offered a broad grin. Gideon, after the exchange of a few words, threw back his head and roared with laughter.

Marti remained standing at the window, certain Gideon couldn't see her. Her standing aside and watching him, wondering about him, was a repeat of the day before. Here, distanced from him once again, she felt something of his raw energy, his excitement. He was a man who lived life to the hilt; he was, she realized, the most attractive man she'd ever met. She felt charged with an expectation that was new to her. But still she didn't move, not quite yet.

She watched as a beautiful young redhead came up to him, drew him aside and put her arms around his neck. For a moment they stood there, noses touching, and talking. Gideon then kissed her quickly and pushed her away with a smile at once charming and yet firm. She walked slowly toward the back of the bar after giving him a reluctant glance, but Gideon had already turned away.

Several people were walking quickly down the street, chatting in low voices, their footsteps heavy on the pavement. Marti turned and watched them for a long moment, feeling unexpectedly alone. She turned back to the scene in the restaurant, wanting without reason to cut and run. The questions she had refused to consider began to surface one after another, questions for which she had no answers.

What in the world was she getting herself into? Why had Gideon so relentlessly tracked her down? How could she be so foolish, so vulnerable to flattery?

A cab drew up. Someone stepped out and went quickly into the restaurant. The scent of liquor and the fragrance of flowers and buttery cooking drifted out over the sound of chatter and laughter.

Gideon stood at the bar now, his back turned to her. *Oh, damn,* Marti thought. She was nervous, yes, and feeling foolish and vulnerable. A handsome man with sapphire eyes had asked her for a date. *You're responsible for your own life,* she told herself. Talley's was a public place, the safest place in the world.

There was something about the man, no matter what her doubts were, that she couldn't walk away from. If she turned her back without finding out more about him, she'd regret it for the rest of her life. She went resolutely over to the door and pushed it to with a firmness she didn't quite feel. Too late to turn back now.

"He-ey," someone said to her in a long, drawn-out invitation. She looked over at the bar, and a tweed-jacketed man with curly gray hair raised a glass in her direction. "Hey, what can I get you?"

"Sorry." She smiled, inclined her head in acknowledgment and waited for Gideon to see her.

"Marti." When she caught his eye, he gave her a dazzling smile. He was with her in an instant, bending over her and placing a kiss on each cheek. "I was beginning to wonder whether you were lost."

He seemed so genuinely pleased to see her that Marti's defenses momentarily dropped away. "I've been running late," she said offhandedly as he drew her over to a crowded table at the rear. The three men at the table got quickly to their feet, smiling benignly at her. The fourth person, sitting on a banquette against the wall, was a small, animated woman with a sharp, pretty face and thick black hair piled artfully on her head.

Gideon grasped Marti's hand warmly, sliding right into the introductions. "Here's Marti Holland, our expert of economics. Perhaps she can tell us where the money's buried." She realized that David Lund was one of the men. Nodding at him, she received a friendly smile in return.

"This is Pilar do Valles," Gideon said. Marti leaned forward and shook a pale, ungiving hand.

"Franta do Valles, her husband. To his right is David Lund, whom you met, and to his right is Alec Keller. All have to do with the movie we're making. And now let me get your coat...."

Gideon helped Marti out of her raincoat. She wore a soft beige jersey dress with a rope of coral beads at her neck. She saw the quick glance Gideon gave her, his eyes lighting with approval. Then he had the waiter bring a chair over to the table. With much maneuvering Gideon seated himself so that his knees touched hers and his arm rested across the back of her chair. "Now, what would you like? Have you had dinner?" She had the curious feeling of being cosseted, as though she were a very valuable piece of china.

There were several half-filled champagne glasses on the table, a bottle of champagne in a bucket and Marti noted, a glass of beer where Gideon sat.

"A beer will do," she said, "and I've had dinner."

Pilar gave Marti a brief, dismissive nod. She turned to Gideon and began at once to talk in rapid-fire English. "So there's no need to have those extras work overtime on the weekend if you just schedule the shooting on Monday. Am I right, Gideon? I mean, that's what you're great at, isn't it? The quick kill? This is the way you do it—pah, pah, pah," she said, hitting her fist into the palm of her hand. "You were with the Mossad once, weren't you, Gideon? Israeli secret intelligence? In and out, one-two-three? Economy of action? Beautiful, beautiful—that's why I wanted you to direct *Checkpoint*." She offered him a smile, which animated her face and made her suddenly quite beautiful. "Tell me you were a member of the Mossad. I'd take that as an omen that this picture will be a success."

Marti felt more than heard his quick intake of breath, and his hand stiffened at her back. "Now, where did you get that notion, Pilar?" he asked in a lazy, pleasant voice.

"It's what I heard," she said, giving him a wily look.

If he objects, Marti thought, *then I'll believe she's speaking the truth.*

Gideon laughed and turned away to catch the waiter's eye. "I haven't ordered your beer yet," he said to Marti.

"It doesn't matter."

"Sure it does. I love beer-guzzling American women. Especially when they're in the economics business. You don't happen to mud wrestle as a hobby, do you?"

Marti laughed. His hand pressed her shoulder and remained there. "I don't guzzle beer; I sip it," she said, feeling unexpectedly light-headed and happy over her decision to come. "And I also don't mud wrestle."

"Pity," he said.

"I could always take it up," she said. "New York has everything. Surely there's a mud-wrestling school somewhere."

David Lund, who had been listening closely, said, "If not, we can always start one." He turned to Pilar. "You had a mud-wrestling scene in one of your movies. We'll want you as chairperson of the education department."

"What are we talking about?" Pilar said. "Doesn't anyone have anything serious to say around here?"

The waiter came by with the beer, and during the flurry of its being served, Gideon spoke into Marti's ear, his breath a warm rustle against her skin. "You wouldn't happen to be a fan of the great Miss Nita Sears?"

Marti found Pilar staring curiously at her, eyes glinting with malice. "What is it you're saying?" the actress demanded. "Speak up, Gideon. I can't hear you."

Nita Sears was a dumpling of a woman who sang thirties songs in a high, sweet voice to her own piano accompaniment. "I adore her," Marti said, turning a surprised look at him.

"Then let's get the hell out of here," he said, pushing back his chair. "Come on: she's singing in a joint near the Waldorf. Pilar," he added, "I'll talk to you tomorrow."

"Gideon." His name was ground out as if it were a command to stay.

Franta do Valles got to his feet when Marti stood up, giving her a small, apologetic smile.

"Tomorrow, Pilar," Gideon said, his hand at Marti's waist, pushing her firmly forward.

While Gideon hailed a cab, Marti said breathlessly, "I don't think Pilar's very happy about this."

A cab drew to a halt beside them. Gideon looked quickly back at her, his mouth drawn into an unexpectedly tight line. "I'm making the film for the lady," he said tersely, "not decorating her bed."

"I didn't mean . . ." she began, embarrassed.

"Come on; get in. I know what you didn't mean."

"Where to?" the cabbie asked.

"East Fifty-fourth and Park, north side. It's called the Cat's Eye. Ever been there?" he asked Marti. "Incidentally, all references to Pilar will be sidelined for the evening. That is an American word, isn't it?"

"Yes, I suppose so. It sounds very political to me. As for the Cat's Eye, no, I've never been there. I've been meaning to," she added, letting her voice drop away. No, she had not been meaning to, not in the literal sense, not in her curiously circumscribed life.

"You've been meaning to," Gideon repeated. "I wonder what keeps you so busy? Besides receptions at the United Nations, that is."

"I'm not always in the country," she said defensively, wondering why she hadn't answered his question with a simple negative.

"Really? And where do your peregrinations take you?"

"Everywhere. India, Africa, Third World countries."

"And what are you an expert on, exactly? You said something yesterday about being on the economics subcommittee."

"Well, I'm an expert on farming, more or less."

His smile was clearly one of admiration. "I'm impressed. Then you're more or less a farm girl."

She laughed. "No, I grew up on the city's streets, right here in New York."

"Parents?"

"Yes, they're retired and live in Florida."

"Brothers? Sisters?"

"One sister with one child."

"And how did you go from the streets of New York to farming?"

"I'm not quite certain," she said with a laugh. "I studied economics at New York University. Then, in a desire to learn something about the land, I took another degree in conservation. When your expertise is arcane, you'd be surprised how quickly people want you for your expert advice."

"I like a modest lady." He picked up her hand, entwining his fingers through hers.

"I thought you liked mud-wrestling, beer-guzzling ladies." She felt a small, warm thread of pleasure at his touch at precisely the same moment that a warning bell went off in her head. She did not attempt to move, however, enjoying the exciting trail along her skin left by his touch.

There was no reason in the world why they should be sitting side by side in a cab on the way to hear Nita Sears sing. The basic question hadn't been answered. Not what was she doing there but why was she there? What did he want?

He released her hand and pulled her close. He felt good—and, she decided, catching the amused eye of the cabbie through his rearview mirror, safe enough for the time being. He pressed his nose against her hair. "I'm beginning to think Nita Sears is a bad idea."

Marti drew away and cast a curious gaze at him. "I never did get a taste of the beer, considering how fast you hustled me out of Talley's. Mind telling me why?"

He reached over and touched her nose. "I think it was the freckles that got me. I knew I had to be alone with them."

"I wonder why I have trouble believing you."

"Oh, ye who have such little faith in lovers of freckles. What else is bothering you?"

She waited a moment before answering. He was staring intently at her, and she saw more than just idle curiosity in his eyes. "What else is bothering me?" she repeated at last. "Why, your coming on to me as strongly as you are."

"Is that what you call it? 'Coming on'?"

"Not the most elegant of phrases, but that's what I call it."

A few seconds passed before he spoke, and when he did, his words took her by surprise. "That's a very strange question. I've just been following through, that's all."

Marti sat bolt upright. "Would you mind making yourself clear?"

"You moved in on Dave and me yesterday at the UN, and I liked it. I like the way you operate. Hello, here I am, who are you? Lovely. No preliminaries, no coy smiles or come-hither looks. Tell me," he said, lifting her chin and looking into her eyes, "did you pick us out of the madding crowd, or did someone send you?"

Marti gasped audibly. His eyes were glittering and clever. She pulled away. "I don't know what you're talking about."

He laughed and leaned back against the seat. "For a while I'd thought that maybe you were a starlet looking for the big break."

"It happens all the time, I suppose," she said coldly.

"So it does."

"And you just stood there, letting the so-called starlet do her stuff."

"Why not? I'm male. I've got all the right parts."

"Irresistible, aren't you?" she said angrily. "Well, perhaps it was David Lund I was after. He is cute and cuddly."

"Point made," he acknowledged, grinning. "Maybe I deserved that."

"It must be wonderful being a movie director. You look for motives where there aren't any, but I suppose that goes with the territory.

"What do you know about my being a movie director?"

"I don't," she said. "I must read about you sometime." She glanced out the window as the cab made the turn and headed south toward Fifty-fourth Street. She remembered with a sudden shock that the Cat's Eye was near the Waldorf and that at about one o'clock that morning a man had plunged to his death. She shuddered faintly as the voice of her telephone caller came back. Marti hadn't been able to shake the sense she'd had all day that Gideon Sanders was somehow involved.

"I'll send you a bookful of clippings," he was saying. "You haven't answered my question."

"I'm sorry," she told him, turning to him and measuring each word. "I've forgotten it already. Would you mind repeating it?"

Gideon smiled and reached into his pocket for the fare as the cab made the turn into Fifty-fourth Street. "We'll get to it by and by," he said.

The Cat's Eye was in a small, pretty hotel just off Park Avenue. Above its entrance from the street was a tiny, amusing neon sign showing a winking cat's eye. Although it was the middle of the week, a late-night crowd had drifted into the small lounge, which held a bar at one end and a dozen tiny tables facing the piano.

"Wonderful," Gideon said as they were shown to the only empty table in the room. "The set hasn't begun yet. Afterward I'll ask her to come by for a drink."

"Where did you hear Nita Sears?" Marti asked. "I thought she was a particularly American phenomenon." The tension between them hadn't quite disappeared, but she was glad of Gideon's attempt to deflect it.

"Oh, I've heard her here, there, everywhere. She was in London last year. I'm figuring on slipping her into the movie I'm making."

"And to think she's not even a starlet!"

"Occasionally I do things just for the artistic hell of it."

Marti flushed, aware that he was not taking his eyes from hers, finding his attention both pleasing and disconcerting.

"When I was in college," she said in order to keep the conversation from becoming intimate, "we collected Nita Sears records, but we could never afford to come to an uptown joint to hear her." Marti remembered warm days in the city when she and her friends would go down to the Village Gate for jazz on Friday nights. One beer coddled at the bar would last them through several sets. Warm days. Free days. Wonderful days.

"Your eyes are lighting up," he said. "With remembrance, I'm led to believe. Anyone I'm supposed to be jealous of?"

"It was a million years ago, Gideon. College, jazz in the Village. We were too poor for Nita Sears, but we managed to hear a lot of jazz. Funny how I've let it all slip away."

He reached over and touched the rope of coral beads she wore. "Ready to tell me about this strange creature who edged her way into my life yesterday at precisely the cocktail hour, not-so-mean Greenwich time?"

She laughed, experiencing a sensation of happiness that was unexpected but which she made no effort to quell.

"Every little cell," he added, "including the DNA."

She took in a deep breath, feeling his hand against her neck. "I want a fair exchange, however," she told him. She reached up and put her hand on his arm.

"Which is?"

"I want to know everything about you, including the Mossad."

For a long moment the silence between them held. She could read nothing in his expression, and then she saw it: the faintest flicker, the warning that she had gone too far. She took her hand from his arm and instinctively reached for the coolness of the small vase that sat in the center of the table, holding a pink rose.

For another second his hand remained against her neck, and then he withdrew it. "You know, when Pilar acts cute, I have to curtail a desire to strangle her. She's the boss lady. I'm still testing my reaction to you."

"You invited me out for tonight. It wasn't the other way around, Gideon. I didn't realize there would be restrictions on what I might or might not be able to say."

"Of course," he agreed tightly. "You're perfectly right. Ask away, and if I can't answer your questions, I'll tell you so right off without the least rancor."

"Sorry," she said, trying to make light of her remark, "but I live in a world that's one part charity, one part hope and one part paranoia. I think we've been into that already." Marti realized she had been longing to talk to him about her threatening telephone call, but she knew she couldn't, not now and possibly not ever. But there was that other business, the Jacques Foliere business.

"I thought about you this morning," she began, choosing her words carefully. "I mean, before you telephoned."

"I must've received your message—the mental one, that is."

"No, it was something else. The diplomat who fell to his death early this morning?"

"Ah." He watched her, his expression unchanged.

"It touched pretty close to home, didn't it? You did say you were on the fifteenth floor of the Waldorf."

"What an extraordinary memory you have," he said.

"Extraordinary? You made it perfectly clear yesterday."

"Ah," he said, "but yesterday I was under your spell. I would've signed away my birthright."

"And today?" she asked.

"Today I've had time to think about you. Marti Holland, I told myself, is soft and sweet and not given to aggressive acts. Therefore, I ask myself, what is she doing in my life and why? The answer is, I'm a film director, and you've something to sell me. But now you've turned the tables by asking me a very unusual question. Unusual, that is for someone who isn't a policeman."

Dangerous ground. She realized that now and was indeed sorry she had stepped there, however carefully. "Just native curiosity, that's all," she said in an offhand manner, hoping it would satisfy him.

He watched her out of narrowed eyes. "Jacques Foliere, the member of UNESCO who went out the window. Is your native curiosity suggesting I helped him on his way?"

The waiter came by, and Gideon, without asking, ordered glasses of white wine as though he were anxious to be rid of him. "Oh," he added, "and please ask Miss Sears if she wouldn't like to have a drink with me after the set. I'm Gideon Sanders." And then, just when he turned back to Marti, there was an enthusiastic round of applause.

A short, plump woman with a mop of dyed blond hair made her way out of the back, wearing a broad grin on a very pretty face. She was swathed in a brightly sequined dress that was meant to hide the fullness of her figure but in fact did more to emphasize it.

She smiled endearingly, thick black lashes framing wide blue eyes. Then she pushed up her long sleeves and sat down at the piano. "Here we are again," she murmured into the mike in a low, seductive voice, unlike that of her high, charmingly affected singing voice. "I thought I'd begin with my favorite, 'Dancing on the Ceiling,' and just go on from there." She looked across the room directly at Gideon and gave him a broad wink. "And a special hello to our friend from across the sea."

Gideon returned the salute with a crooked grin. When he turned back to Marti, his face still wore the grin, and as they both applauded the singer enthusiastically, Marti felt the tension leave the air.

The set might have lasted forty minutes or an hour. Marti wasn't aware of time; all that existed was the high, sweet voice singing a variety of songs of the thirties as well as several patter songs that had been written especially for Nita Sears.

When it was over, the singer came to their table, trailing a heavy, pleasant floral scent.

"Gideon," she said, allowing him to plant a kiss on each cheek, "how's the movie business? I've been reading about you in the papers."

"I'm going to fit you into *Checkpoint*," he said. "Nita, meet Marti Holland, who's a fan of yours."

Nita put a plump hand out and held Marti's for a long moment before sitting down. "Any fan of mine is a friend of mine," she said. "You in pictures, too?"

"Marti's with the UN," Gideon put in. "What would you like to drink?"

"Diet soda," the singer responded with a chuckle. "If I'm going to be in the movies, I'd better take off a couple of pounds. The UN, huh? Sounds fascinating. What do you do at the UN, Marti?"

"She's an economics adviser," Gideon said.

"Hey, let the lady speak."

Marti laughed, enjoying herself and even Gideon's proprietary attitude. "I'm an economics adviser."

"Whatever that is," Nita said. "No, don't tell me. I may learn something, and at my age that can be treacherous."

The singer stayed with them for another five minutes, talking about the scene Gideon planned to film of her singing in the club. "Hey," she said, turning to Marti, "make him give you a part, too. He's the dispenser of that kind of largess. You'd be surprised how being a movie star can enhance your career."

Marti laughed. "At the UN?"

"Sure, honey. There's no biz like show-and-tell biz." Nita Sears ingested the diet soda in a long swig and then got slowly to her feet. "Well, I need my rest. Thanks for the drink." She leaned toward Gideon to give and receive a farewell kiss. Then she turned to Marti and held out her hand. "You make a star out of her, you hear?" She threw a stern look at Gideon.

"If that's what she wants."

When the singer had gone, Marti turned to him. "It's all right; you don't have to worry. I don't have an Actor's Equity card."

"Maybe I'd like to show you off," he commented.

Before Marti could say anything, Gideon surprisingly brought up the subject of Jacques Foliere again. "I'm still interested in why you connected me with Foliere."

"I didn't connect you—at least, not in the way you mean," she said, stumbling over her words. "It struck me when I read about it."

"What, precisely, struck you?"

"Well for one thing, I knew Jacques Foliere. Slightly, I mean," she added hastily. "Actually," she continued with a qualifying sigh, "we met briefly for the first time yesterday, although we'd been corresponding about the project I'm working on."

"You seem to have met everyone briefly yesterday," he remarked a little coldly.

"And then..."

"And then I, by a twist of fate," he took up, unable to hide the anger in his voice, "happened to have a suite on the fifteenth floor of the hotel out of which Foliere chose to plunge to his death. From the fifteenth floor. Therefore, I must know something about it. The fact that dozens of other citizens also occupied the same floor but are unknown to you means nothing. The fact that I'm from that tough little nation across the seas means I'm up to something, something bold and beyond the law. The quick kill in the night that silences the enemy. Oh, lady," he said, shaking his head as he reached for her hand. Cupping it between his own, he drew it to his lips. "What kind of dreams do you have at those council meetings when the speakers blow windy and long?" The touch of his lips against her palm was warm, sending long, lovely tremors through her body.

"Don't," she said in a whisper, the word coming uninvited. When he gave her an impatient smile, she protested, "I thought nothing of any kind, just of coincidence."

"Just coincidence."

"Pure and simple."

"Then, Marti, I'm going to believe you."

"Very clever of you to back me up against a wall and then forgive me for something for which I need no forgiveness."

He laughed and once more gently kissed the palm of her hand. "I suppose you'd consider my digs at the Waldorf off-limits—strictly for fooling around, I mean."

She was aware of watching his mouth, of wanting it pressed against hers. When she spoke, it was to chase away the sensual strain she felt coursing through her body, as though mere words could do it. "I'm not a starlet in search of a job. Remember that, Gideon."

"I know you're not a starlet. You're entirely too argumentative. You haven't touched your wine. We're going to have to start worrying soon that you'll die of dehydration."

"Not interested," she told him. She thought, with the most reckless abandon, that she wanted him, that she wanted his lips on hers and his arms around her and that she had never had such an intense feeling before. She was startled once again by the clarity of his eyes and how easily she could be taken in by them.

"Where did you say you live?" he asked.

"I somehow think you know," she remarked. "There's a lot we haven't said to one another, isn't there?"

"Yes." He signaled for the check and then signed for it when it arrived. When he turned back, he said, "Marti Holland," as though it were a complete statement in itself. He waited for the space of a second or two. "I'm still trying to figure you out."

"What are you talking about?" she asked, feeling the first pangs of alarm.

"Yesterday you picked Dave and me out of the crowd in what I perceived to be a carefully calculated manner. I bit, and you knew I would. That's pretty clever planning. Either you know everything about me, while I know nothing about you . . ."

"Now it's nothing, is it?" she said, keeping her voice calm but feeling her heart hammering wildly. "I'd say you bit in a very calculated way, if that's what you think I did."

"Didn't you?" He smiled and reached over for her hand. "Come on, soldier. I don't trust that innocent, wide-eyed look you're giving me. I promise you one thing, though. Before this evening is over, I'm going to find out what makes Marti Holland tick."

Chapter Five

"Come on; it's a fine night for walking," Gideon said, taking her hand again as they emerged on the sidewalk. The air, which was still and warm, possessed a faint crisp edge—a reminder that it was late autumn and there was no arguing about the inevitability of winter. "What do they call this weather? Indian summer? Any idea why?" he asked.

"None at all," said Marti. "I told you, I'm a city kid. The questions I ask are of a different nature."

"Ah, you just take it for granted that an unexpected warm spell in the late fall is called Indian summer, but 'why' isn't in your lexicon. Amazing, you Americans. You take entirely too much for granted. Madison Avenue is that way," he added, pointing west, "and Park Avenue is east, if I'm not mistaken. You're east."

"So I am. And amazing, you Israelis. You jump to quick conclusions. You're very ancient and very brand-new and very sure of yourselves. You haven't a minute to waste, and you think we're all quite overweight with the good life. Worse, you think we're profligate and have no idea of our good fortune. You're wrong, you know, all wrong."

"Come on, economist," he said, tugging her along in the direction of Park Avenue. "Maybe I deserved that, but maybe being feisty and self-assured is in our nature, ingested along with mother's milk.''

"Gideon!" There was an imperative note in her tone that made him stop and look quizzically at her. "Just a minute," Marti said. "You've manipulated this evening very nicely so far. When is it my turn?"

"Have I really given you anything to complain about?"

"Gideon, everything."

"What is it?" he asked in a softened tone, although he was aware of both the air of resilience that she projected and a certain toughness. He had no doubt that it was time to clear up a number of puzzling questions about the lady. He was, however, uncertain whether this was the time or place for it.

"Was Pilar right?" she asked. "Are you in the Mossad?"

The question was as swiftly thrown at him as a right jab to the jaw. His reaction was no less swift. He reached out and gripped her shoulders between strong hands, feeling a faint shudder race through her. "I thought we dispensed with that question some time ago."

"But we haven't," Marti said. "You're a genius at equivocation, Gideon. I have to know."

"Do you, now?"

"Gideon, don't treat me in that amused, superior way."

"Is that what you call it? Pilar's a damn fool, and she says anything that comes into her head."

"Gideon," she implored, "you're fudging again. I don't care about Pilar one way or the other."

He dropped his hands away and turned from her, striding quickly down the street. It was nearing midnight and quiet. He heard her heels tapping lightly on the sidewalk as she ran to catch up with him. He stopped and waited, his hands clenched deep in his pants pockets.

"Something happened today," she told him simply.

"I see." Coldly he turned to her, holding his anger back. "A man fell from the fifteenth floor of my hotel. Therefore, being Israeli and a tough hombre all around, I killed him. Having killed him, it stands to reason that I'm with the Mossad. Lady, the best thing I can do for you is to put you in a cab and send you back to whatever dreary, unforgiving life you lead."

For a long moment she stared at him. Her lips, slightly moist, were parted. He read the hurt and bravery in her eyes, and in a second it was all over. He reached for her and enveloped her in his arms. "What is it?"

"A whole bunch of things," she said against his chest. "It's getting on a roller-coaster ride and not being able to get off. Just tell me you're Gideon Sanders and that you're making a film and that's it. When the film is over, you'll pack up and go wherever it is film directors go."

He was a long time answering. He thought of David Lund's incredulity: "Assassin? Marti Holland!" To David it seemed impossible. But not to Gideon. Everything is possible in this most impossible of worlds was Gideon's credo. "You're asking me a question that shouldn't be asked, ever. FBI, CIA, KGB, CID, the Mossad—what the devil do you think they mean? In your life, nothing. Nothing. And absolutely nothing to do with you and me. Come on; let's walk."

"It's not a dumb question, Gideon. I merely want your assurance— Oh, you wouldn't give it to me, anyway."

"Marti, my underground activities are confined to my movies." He draped his arm lightly across her shoulders and directed her gently along. "Do you feel you're in possession of some special knowledge of me that the police don't already have?"

He heard the faint gasp and then the too-quick response. "I've no idea what the police know."

And you, my pretty one, he thought, *won't hear it from me.* "The police," he told her carefully, "questioned me. They questioned everybody, including the lady who places a chocolate on my pillow every night. Satisfied with that explanation?"

She looked queryingly up at him. "Have I a choice?"

"None whatsoever. Mind telling me why you need any special assurance about me?"

Marti ignored the question. She had to think, to make decisions. "Let's walk along here," she said, turning left on Park Avenue. "Do you know the Plaza fountain?"

"I do indeed. We did some shooting there, as a matter of fact." He kept his arm draped casually across her shoulders, drawing her close.

Briefly Marti closed her eyes, letting the sensation of his touch wash over her. Why couldn't she just get on with the evening and treat it merely as a date with an attractive man, period?

But no, it was impossible. She felt a certain distrust on his part, too; he hadn't bought her coming up to him at the reception just to pass the time of day. Then what could he be thinking of her? She had no idea.

They were circling each other warily, and Marti had three strikes against him that she couldn't ignore. His remark about Sheikh Hikmat was the first. The second was Jacques Foliere's falling to his death. And last there was the telephone call. Who had made it? Who had wanted to scare her into silence?

Park Avenue, with its center dividing island filled with trees and autumn flowers, was quiet, as though settled in for the night. The few pedestrians who happened along glanced at them, looking quickly away as though eye contact were too risky in that city of imponderables.

Live for the moment, whispered the unbidden little voice that seemed to have taken over her life. *At least such a mo-*

ment as this. Park Avenue with a handsome man on a warm Indian-summer night. It was enough; really it was.

Trust, lack of trust. Maybe she was imagining things. Maybe he was interested in her, really interested, man-woman interested. It occurred to her that her outlook was still entirely too serious. In a moment of daring, as they turned west on Fifty-eighth Street, she curled her arm along his waist. "The question, *cher maître*," she said, adopting a lighter tone, "is about the movie you're making. *Checkpoint*. Sounds ominous."

"The only thing ominous in the movie is its star and producer, Pilar do Valles. Her husband's company is the chief backer, which means she's double trouble."

"Double?"

"It's not enough that she has the unqualified backing of a large corporation with money to spend. She's also a genuine star. You know, complete with bright lights and trumpet fanfare?"

"She's an odd-looking little thing," Marti commented in an admiring way. "I saw her in *Carnival*. She was quite beautiful."

"Light and shadow, that's all. The camera knows precisely what to make of her. I wish," he added with a slight laugh, "I did."

"She's rather possessive about you."

The remark took Gideon by surprise. He stopped in the middle of the street, scarcely aware of a group of people coming at them who had to separate and move around them. "Women will never fail to amaze me," he said, looking down at her with an admiring smile. "Now, what made you come to that conclusion?"

Marti shrugged. He felt her slender arms under the soft, pliant stuff of her raincoat. "Mostly by the way she totally ignored me," she said.

"And I've an uncommon urge not to ignore you," he said, running his finger down her forehead and over the tip of her nose, "Pilar be damned." He could smell her perfume. It was heady, reminiscent of some desert flower he couldn't name. They stood for a long moment gazing at each other, Gideon troubled by the unexpected flood of raw desire he felt for her.

He was going off the mark, he thought, being twisted either by a pro or by something ineffably sweet and good. "Come on," he said huskily, tucking his arm through hers. "Steady progress is necessary at this point in our relationship."

"Relationship! Is that what you call it?" Marti gave a brief laugh. Gideon detected something pleased, even tender, in her tone, something that emphasized her vulnerability. An inner voice told him to get on with it, that it was not exactly playtime.

She joined her stride to his. "About *Checkpoint*," she reminded him. "You're not shooting right now, are you? I mean, I thought when a picture was in the process of being made, visits to Talley's and intimate nightclubs wouldn't be quite in the mode."

"You've been reading too many movie magazines. Pilar never minds a little extra exposure. Anyway, the truth is, we've hit a snag here," he said. "The major portion of the filming, fortunately, was done abroad, especially in North Africa."

She was a long time asking the question, and when she did, Gideon noted hesitancy in her tone. "Exactly what is the plot?"

"No secret about it. It's one of those lovely plots you can define in a sentence: the sudden death of a sheikh and the repercussions it has in the Mideast power struggle."

Marti put her hand to her mouth and then suddenly stumbled. It was only his grasp on her arm that prevented her from falling. "I'm sorry," she said, hopping on one foot and briefly rubbing her ankle. "My heel caught."

"Any damage?"

"Let's see." Marti held on to his arm and took her shoe off. She examined the heel carefully, showing it to him. There were no scuff marks or breaks. "Lucky me," she said, offering him a brave, apologetic smile. "Nothing happened. My heel hit a break in the pavement, I think."

Gideon looked back at the smooth flow of pavement. There were no cracks, banana peels or even discarded cigarette wrappers that would have caused her to lose her balance in quite that way. "As long as you're all right. Do you want me to call a cab?"

"No, no," she said hastily. "Nothing's wrong. I'm fine."

And methinks, he told himself, *the lady protests too much.* But once more he tucked his arm through hers, carefully reaching for her hand. "Come on, then, if you're sure."

"I'm sure."

The park loomed up ahead. Its trees, denuded of leaves, were calligraphic strokes against the late-night sky.

"Is it Israelis against the Arabs?" Marti asked quietly.

"Are we back to that?"

"I'm just curious, Gideon, really."

"Haven't you heard," he responded after a moment, "working at the United Nations as you do, that there's reconciliation in the air? What we're making is a star vehicle for Pilar do Valles, not a political tract. It's an excellent script, packed with dynamite. Plenty of suspense. The setting is the United Nations and the Middle East."

"Good guys, bad guys not defined exactly," Marti said.

"Exactly."

"But part of it," Marti pursued, "takes place at UN headquarters, except that you haven't received permission to film there."

Gideon gave her a surprised look. She had inadvertently fed something to him, something that was not quite common knowledge. Unless, of course, the chief of security at the UN, Reed Douglas, had told her. "You're a fountain of information," he remarked. "What else have you got to tell me?"

She turned quickly away. If he could examine her closely, he speculated, he would find the color rushing to her cheeks. "At the UN they're talking of nothing else," she said. "It's not every day that a famous movie director shows up wanting to make a film there."

"Really?" He was quiet for a while, waiting for her to make another slip. "I had the impression that film directors are turned away daily."

"This is a bad time of the year," she told him.

"Right," he said. "Like oysters out of season. I understand."

"What do you propose to do about it, then?" she asked.

"Wing it, as you Americans say."

They reached Fifth Avenue and crossed over to the Plaza fountain. They stopped to admire the statue of Persephone perched above, carrying a jar of water that spilled endlessly into the basin below.

"The fountain will be turned off for the winter," Marti said, "but then they'll string her with a waterfall of Christmas lights."

"Ever toss any pennies into it?" Gideon asked.

"When I was a down-and-out college student, we once spent an hour trying to fish them out. My share was a dollar and a quarter before some spoilsport of a cop told us to get lost."

"His territory, no doubt."

"We had it down to a science, too," Marti went on.

"Is that why you became an economist, all that high finance?"

There was a black-garbed mime sitting on the fountain basin. His face was painted a stark white, broken only by a slash of red across his lips and a vertical black line bisecting each eye. When he saw Marti and Gideon, he sprang to life, imitating a dog straining at a leash.

"A mime at midnight," Gideon said. "Doesn't New York ever sleep?"

"There's one mime that doesn't. Maybe he didn't make his quota today. Maybe he's lonely."

They stood watching him for a while along with several other passersby. Gideon fished for some change in his pocket and came up with a couple of dollars when the mime passed his battered top hat around.

"He can go home now," Marti said.

They walked across Fifty-ninth Street to reach Central Park, where Gideon asked her the question once again. "About your becoming an economist, did it all start there at the Plaza fountain?"

They were walking along the park now, on the Fifth Avenue side, where the length of the park was bordered by a stone wall.

"No, it all started with my having parents who gave me lessons in everything from the violin to ice-skating."

Gideon grinned and shook his head. "I see, the man said with an air of not understanding at all."

"Do you have siblings?"

"Three—two brothers and one sister. I'm the middle son."

"Ah, then perhaps you know nothing of having every wish anticipated because you're the youngest. Such as when I showed a gift for drawing, I was immediately packed off to art class. When I came home with good grades in math, I was lectured on the virtues of a life in science."

"Then how, given the choices," he said, following her over to a bench, where she sat down and slipped off her shoes, "did you end up in whatever it is you do in higher economics?"

"I like it," she said simply, wriggling her toes in the air. "I was nurtured on discipline, on the advantages of mastering a difficult subject, on making a good life for myself."

He sat down next to her. "And you've succeeded."

She was slow in answering. "Certainly I've succeeded," she agreed finally, and then added, as though something within her might argue the point, "remarkably well."

"No wishes, regrets or desires?"

"None whatsoever, except that we stop playing twenty questions." She slipped her shoes back on, got up quickly and began walking away.

No, she did not like twenty questions any more than he, and she did not want to discuss a life lived decidedly too much in a mold. She continued walking parallel to the stone wall, past empty benches and an occasional pedestrian with a dog. Cars proceeded smoothly along the avenue without the usual daytime tie-ups and horn blowing, as if out of consideration for those asleep in the stately buildings opposite.

She heard Gideon's footsteps and then felt his hand on her arm. For some reason, the quiet action frightened her. "You scared the devil out of me," she said sharply.

"Marti." The simple command was given in a low voice that forced her to slacken her pace. "I've a strange notion that we're being followed. Two men behind us are entirely too interested in who we are and where we're going."

She stopped and started to turn around, only to feel Gideon's fingers dig into her arm.

"That's right; let them know you're interested in them. Don't be such a bloody little fool."

Marti pulled back, regarding him with suspicion. She had lived in New York for most of her life, and she'd learned a few lessons about confronting danger. "Stop playing games, Gideon. You've taken it on yourself to add what you think is adventure to the evening. You needn't. I've had enough for a lifetime, thank you." When she saw the look of dark anger on his face, she added, suddenly not at all sure of herself, "How do you know they're following us?"

"They picked us up when we left the Cat's Eye and have been behind us with a slow, steady pace ever since."

"And you're just telling me now?"

"I can't stop two mugs from taking a leisurely walk."

"Let's grab a cab and get out of here," she said, her heart beginning to race.

"Then we'll never know, and I hate to leave things undone. Come over here," he said, taking her elbow and guiding her to the stone wall. "Right here should do it." He pulled her behind a huge old sycamore that hid them from view. Marti had a glimpse of two fit young men in jeans and bomber jackets about fifty feet behind them.

"Gideon, I'm not prepared for a mugging in Central Park at midnight," she told him. "Let's grab a cab."

"There won't be any mugging, believe me. Just play it my way for a while." In a moment he had pulled her close, his lips on hers, pressing, urging them apart.

"Gideon," she said, tearing away. "Are you mad?"

He gave a quick, longing look at her lips and then said roughly, "Stay here. Don't move."

She was aware of a stretch of silence, as if the traffic had melted away and they inhabited a ghost town. The two figures had stopped and were in the process of lighting cigarettes, one offering a match to the other.

Gideon remained standing without moving in the shadow of the tree. When the match flared, he surveyed their profiles quickly. Young anonymous punks. Sent to do the job or out to make a few easy bucks. Gideon had no idea which.

He stepped out from behind the tree, his muscles taut and ready. "Got a match?"

Their response was a long curse in French. He understood it well. They moved fast, and the cigarette flipped away, describing an arc and landing at the curb. Gideon, feet splayed apart, understood the element of surprise better than they, however. They approached swinging, certain they had fear on their side. It took little more to disarm them. Gideon pulled his punch, swinging right and catching the shorter off guard. Then, with a swift move, he slammed their heads together.

Marti came rushing toward him, holding her bag by its straps, feeling the anger surge in her throat, ready for anything. She heard the sound of screeching wheels and looked thankfully for help. It was a cab coming to a halt, the driver leaning across the front seat to gape.

"Come on," she called to Gideon, who was in the act of hauling one of the hoodlums to his feet. "Let's get out of here."

He thought better of it and pushed the man back down. Punks, maybe. He'd get little out of them. He ran over to the cab and climbed in after Marti. "I should have had them both run in," he said, turning to her and letting out a deep breath.

"Where to?" the cabbie inquired, pointedly not asking any questions although his eyes were alight with curiosity.

"East Eighty-ninth between Second and First; I'll tell you when," Marti said. She turned worriedly to Gideon, although there wasn't a mark on him. "Are you all right?"

When he nodded, she added, "I guess it was all that commando training."

"If that's what you want to call all that time in the army. A lucky punch is how I'd put it." He leaned back against the seat and briefly closed his eyes as the cab pulled away from the curb. Punks or otherwise, he couldn't afford to get involved in a brouhaha.

Marti looked out the rear window. Both men were trudging off slowly in the opposite direction.

"They're not following us, at any rate," she said, relieved. "Why did you take them on like that? We could've gotten rid of them very simply by calling a cab. It's not exactly the least populated part of town."

He opened his eyes and smiled at her. "Just a bit of showing off in front of my girl," he said, "that's all."

Marti leaned back against the seat, as well, her face inches from his. "Liar," she breathed.

He laughed. "You're getting me into a lot more trouble than I bargained for."

"That long curse in French," she said calmly, trying to catch him off guard with her remark. He had acted too quickly, too willingly; he knew too much. "Did you understand it?"

"Certainly," he responded without hesitation. "What surprises me is that you did. It's not precisely the language of the diplomatic front parlor. You're a bundle of contradictions, my girl." He reached for her hand, proceeding to warm it between his own. "Come on; I just saved your life. Level with me. That wasn't an ordinary, everyday mugging. They weren't after me for a bit part in *Checkpoint*, either. What are you up to? If it's something to do with Jacques Foliere..."

"What am I up to?" she asked in surprise. She hadn't thought—but of course it was possible. "I've no idea who they are, and no reason to. You set up the situation and then went in swinging, just to show off.''

She pulled her hand away. ''It's getting chilly. Indian summer is over.'' She understood it now. It didn't take a master's in economics to figure it out. While he couldn't possibly have seen her in the delegates' lounge, couldn't possibly have known she'd heard his conversation, he was curious about her, and it was in connection with her job. The idea made her shiver.

Worse, he didn't trust her, didn't believe she had moved in on him innocently.

The cab was heading across town with a smooth rapidity, lights miraculously turning green at every corner.

Gideon looked over at her with a smile turned knowing. ''I just bashed in a couple of heads on your account. Tell me about you and Jacques Foliere.''

She looked sharply across at him. ''I don't know what you're talking about.''

''You were with him at the Moroccan shindig yesterday. Don't bother denying it, because David Lund saw you there. What were you and he talking about?''

''You and David were discussing me!'' she spluttered. ''How dare you?''

He laughed. ''That's a new one, Marti. How dare I discuss a beautiful woman with my close friend?''

''Okay, okay, I'm being touchy. What were Jacques Foliere and I talking about?'' It was complicated, and she wondered how she might sum it up. ''The drought in Africa and how to start the machinery working again, if it's ever possible. He was an expert on farming in the Sahel.'' She gave a small, embittered laugh. ''What there is left of farming there.''

''So you sit in your comfortable offices,'' he said, gazing out the window, ''or meet over an expense-account lunch and devise new methods.'' The cab swerved onto Third

Avenue and tore uptown. "I suspect he was a man of many parts, your friend Jacques."

"I think you knew him, too," she said, more for effect than because of any belief in what she was saying. She was, therefore, taken aback when he stiffened slightly.

"I read the papers, Marti."

"Then your interest in him is rather curious."

"Only insofar as we were just attacked by two men speaking his native tongue."

"With accents that are more of the North African coast than of France."

He gave a low whistle of admiration. "You're very clever," he told her. "I'm wondering if we shouldn't go to the police with this little problem, after all."

"Lovely. I've a few things I could tell them. In fact, I believe they're probably looking for me."

They were silent after that, each gazing out of the cab window at the quiet city. "That's my street coming up," Marti said a few minutes later. She leaned forward and signaled the driver to stop.

Before she got out, she said to Gideon, "Look, I live partway down the block. I'm not certain whether I want you to do any more than walk me to my front door, and maybe not even that."

"Come on," he said, tucking one arm through hers and opening the door with the other. "You're going to have to trust someone, and it might as well be yours truly."

"I don't trust you," she said as they began to move along the sidewalk. "For all I know, you took on a couple of respectable citizens just to prove some point. I don't know why you phoned me..."

"If you don't, then I'm going to feel a little sorry for you."

"This is where I live," she said, coming to a stop in front of her building. "Good night, Gideon." She ran up the steps lightly, aware of Gideon following close behind her. "Thanks for the interesting evening." She held her hand out and at the same time turned and glanced cautiously into the lighted hall beyond. The door was locked, but someone could be standing there out of sight.

"Marti, I'll see you to your door," Gideon said, watching her hands as she picked nervously at the thin leather straps of her shoulder bag. "You still think I'm responsible for Foliere's death, don't you?"

"No, no, of course not," she protested. "Yes— Oh, I don't know what I think. It's that telephone call to my office this morning. It scared the hell out of me."

He reached out for her arm. His voice was sharp. "What call?"

"I don't know, Gideon. Forget what I said." She berated herself for the slip. Maybe Gideon had been her mysterious caller, after all.

He shook her roughly by the shoulders. "What call?"

"I said forget it. Nothing happened." And if he had been the caller, then he knew about it, anyway.

He stared at her for a long moment, his face cast into a sharp shadow by the light easing out of the front lobby. The cat was out of the bag, after all, or at least some of it, and she felt a curious sense of release. "I got a telephone call at the office this morning," she began without further prompting. "It was a pleasant enough voice, soft and familiar, in the sense that he was friendly, as though we knew each other. Oh, and with a faint accent. Maybe...no, I can't say for certain what kind of accent. Not British, not French, not Italian, not German." She shook her head. "I can only tell you what it was not. Anyway, he thanked me, first of all. Said they appreciated the favor I'd done them. Then he said they would return the favor by not..." She stopped, wondering if she had just made the most horrendous mistake of her life.

"By not what?" he prodded gently.

"By not killing me."

He was silent, gazing curiously at her, as though he would dissect her if he could, while her fingers continued to pick at the straps of her bag.

"Then he said," she continued in a flat voice, "that if I want to stay alive, I should keep it to myself."

"Keep what?" he asked.

She bit her lip. "Gideon, I don't know."

"Did he mention Foliere by name?"

She thought for a moment and then shook her head slowly. "No, he didn't. Actually, I mentioned him. It was something he said, though. Oh, of course!" she cried suddenly, remembering at last. "He said something about a fall from the fifteenth floor being a long way down."

"And you connected it immediately?"

"I'd just been reading about it in the newspaper. Anyway," she added, feeling a little ashamed, "I thought of the Waldorf and you on the fifteenth floor, and that sealed it in my mind."

"Thanks for thinking of me," he said in an acerbic tone. "And have you talked to anyone else?"

"About the telephone call? No, I decided it was a crank call. I've had to field them before. Some people think we're doing too much and threaten us with bodily harm, and some people think we're not doing enough and threaten us with bodily harm. I thought about talking to our security chief but didn't. I suppose I should have called the police, told Virginia, done something, but it happened so quickly, and then there was the meeting and Virginia talking sixteen to the dozen. So much talk and gab and things going on that by the end of the day I decided it was a crank call, period. After all, I had got safely through the day, hadn't I?"

"Till now."

"Till now," she echoed, frowning, afraid that he wasn't taking her seriously. "And I'm still not certain. I only met Foliere once, yesterday, and talked to him for a quarter of an hour, maybe even less."

"And left with him."

"Yes—well, no, I didn't leave with him. We went out the door together, that's all."

"Tell me again what you talked about."

"Nothing, Gideon, believe me. Just the project we were both working on, lunch—" she shrugged "—everyday nonsense. I knew about him, of course, but that was the first time we met, and then only because Virginia didn't want to handle it herself. She talks to the heads of committees, and I get everybody else."

"Virginia." Gideon rolled the word off his tongue as though he might somehow learn something from it. "That's the lanky, officious woman who dragged you away just when the party was getting good."

Marti gave him a grateful smile. If he was her enemy, he was also the world's most charming liar.

They were silent for a while, Gideon gazing thoughtfully at her. From somewhere far away they heard the long, low sound of a police siren. A couple of teenagers walked rapidly by, one of them carrying a huge portable radio loudly tuned to a rock station. The music crackled out at them, then gradually faded away. A breeze stirred up and with the gentlest of whispers breathed a lock of hair over Gideon's eyes. Without even thinking about it, Marti reached up and brushed it back. "I looked for you at the party, but you were gone."

"I had an appointment," he said simply. "It's good to know you were looking for me. Rather gets me off the hook for calling you today and asking for a date." He caught up her hand between his own. "Think, Marti. Your caller's remark indicated that you had somehow fingered Jacques

Foliere." He felt her hand go limp, and in spite of the soft lighting, he knew that she had paled visibly.

"It's true, then, is it?" she asked. "You seem more certain than I."

"You only have two choices. Either you received a threatening telephone call this morning, or you're the victim of a prank—a sick one, maybe, but a prank nonetheless."

"And you think I should let it go at that."

"I didn't say that, Marti."

She opened her bag and reached for her keys. "What about you?" she asked, throwing the question at him while searching for the front-door key. "Do you have a connection with Foliere? What did you tell the police? After all, you were right there, almost at the scene of the crime."

"I talked to them and told them the truth." He reached over and took the keys from her hand. "That I saw nothing, heard nothing and therefore could tell them nothing."

She had no idea whether he was telling the truth but still suddenly regretted having blurted out the story of her telephone call.

"It's a wonder I didn't see it in the headlines: 'Famous Director Quizzed in Death of Diplomat,'" she said, hoping that her sarcasm was not lost on him.

"As long as they spell my name right." He opened the door and followed her in, but before she began the climb up the stairs, he pulled her around. "I don't want you in any danger," he said. "You know that."

"Who are you exactly?" she asked quietly. "You're not just directing a movie, are you? You're used to playing cat and mouse, being in the Mossad and all that." She tried to pull away, but his arms tightened around her. "Is that why you called me this morning?" she said at last. "Invited me to Talley's?"

"You don't see anything," Gideon said, ignoring her question and putting his mouth softly against hers.

She closed her eyes, feeling the warmth trail through her body, knowing his kiss was less hungry than loving and wondering how he could have accomplished it in such a short time. The very beauty of it spelled danger. She pulled away. "Good night, Gideon."

"Why did you decide to trust me," he asked in a quiet voice, "and then back away?"

"I didn't. I haven't. I don't like the fact that you called me because you wanted to learn something. Quote, 'I'm convinced we have a date for tonight . . .' Liar."

"Marti, if I can believe you, someone called you this morning and thanked you for your help in disposing of Jacques Foliere. Why would anyone do that? Obviously he knows you've no idea who he is. Otherwise you would have been put out of the way, too. He was bragging, both over what he had done and over the fact that he let you off. Except that if he wants you, he'll find you. I want you to be afraid—and to stay afraid."

She sighed. "Okay, I'm afraid. I've been scared all day. And I'm scared of you. It's just that I've been too busy to let go. What do you want me to do, call the police?"

He jangled the keys. "Which one is it?"

"Come here." She grabbed them and selected the right one, but before she could thrust them back at him, they heard heavy footsteps clattering down the stairs. Marti instinctively moved against the wall when a young man appeared at the head of the stairs. He saw them and ducked his head. There was something about the look in his glistening eyes that frightened her. She didn't realize she had dropped the keys until Gideon bent down to retrieve them. The man continued running down the stairs. When he passed them, he deliberately pushed himself against Marti, knocking her into Gideon.

He was gone through the lobby door before they could recover. Gideon took off after him, shouting a string of curses. She heard a car door slam outside and wheels screeching as it moved away from the curb.

Gideon came rushing back. "A dark-blue Pontiac. Did you know him?"

"Never saw him before in my life."

"Come on. What floor did you say you live on?"

"Top."

He held on to the keys, and when they arrived at her apartment, he carefully examined both locks before inserting the key. She heard the soft, familiar click as the first bolt slid back. With the second lock undone, he slowly pushed the door open. "If that was an intruder," Gideon said, "he was certainly cautious about locking the door behind him."

He slipped into the apartment, waiting a long moment, listening and watching.

"Marti, don't move." Gideon reached into his jacket pocket and then thought better of it. For a moment he remained very still, listening, sensing, feeling for danger. No sound issued from inside the apartment. He reached for his key chain and the small flashlight it contained. Then he entered the apartment silently, moving on light feet. Quickly and quietly in the dark, using only the small pinpoint beam, he made a quick round of the rooms. The air was warm, smelling faintly of steam heat and tobacco. Did she smoke?

Living room, two small bedrooms, pocket kitchen and bath, closets bursting with clothes. No one.

Marti waited outside, her raincoat pulled tight around her. She could think of nothing but the image of that figure on the staircase. Who was he? Where had he come from? She tried to remember a car outside her building that might have had someone sitting in it but couldn't. She'd been too preoccupied with Gideon.

Then the light went on in the foyer. "Preliminaries over with," Gideon said, coming back. "You're safe enough." He took her arm and led her into the apartment, but before she was over the doorsill, she saw the expression on his face change.

"What is it?" She tore out of his grasp and followed his gaze with her eyes. There on the mirror in her foyer was the message written in large red letters: "Your turn now." Her lipstick lay on the table below, broken in half.

Gideon took his eyes off the words and watched Marti Holland carefully. What was she up to? Had he just walked into a trap?

Chapter Six

The phone had a rather pleasant ring. Nevertheless, it sent a jarring note into the dark; the only light in the room came from a cigarette glowing in an ashtray. Beyond, through half-closed blinds, lay the sleeping city, cushioned by the long, low hum of never-ceasing traffic.

After the third ring the receiver was picked up cautiously. "Yes?"

There was the usual crackling, coughing and misdirecting that meant the call, as expected, was from overseas. Thin glass wires bundled along the ocean bed, afire with pulses of light, hadn't meant a damn. A simple phone call from the European continent was still hit-and-miss technology.

The voice that at last came through was the usual accented growl. It sounded far away at first and then suddenly came in very clearly, as though the call were being made from the room next door. "Nine-seven-eight Bear. Do you read me? Nine-seven-eight Bear."

Code names. They meant business but took delight in code names. Why not Schmidt? Why not Ataturk, Ali Baba, Prince Charles? If the U.S. government was listening in, a zooful of names would intrigue them mightily. But the consortium meant business, deadly business, and questioning policy was no way to get ahead in that particular world.

"Are you there? I said nine-seven-eight Bear."

A deep sigh in response. "Forty-four three Rabbit here."

"What's this about Fox?"

Fox. Foliere. They knew everything. Good. The sooner the better. It was clear they'd already met, then. Seven angry elders in Switzerland around a dark mahogany table plotting strategy; it was there in Bear's tone.

"Mind telling me what happened? Why weren't you on the phone at once?"

"I figured the international wire services would tell you what happened far more easily than I ever could with this arcane method you've hatched."

"Get on with it," the growl demanded.

The receiver was damp with sweat. Rabbit switched hands. "Fox was lured from his lair and had to be dispatched. That's all there was to it."

"Was it a woman?"

"I'm not certain what you mean, friend Bear."

"This lure you're talking about. The news wires told nothing, just that the Fox met his death."

Rabbit reached for the cigarette in the ashtray, using it to light a new one. "The dogs were on his trail. He left a strong scent."

"What dogs? What is this stupidity? Fox was the coolest, smartest operator in the business. What's happening there? We can't afford to have anything go wrong. There's too much riding on this."

Rabbit swore on a long exhalation of breath. Too much riding on it. The consortium met, made decisions, pushed buttons, corrupted the desperate to carry out their plans. And grew fitful when the Jacques Folieres of the world suddenly failed them.

Foliere was the perfect case in point. He held a high position in UNESCO and appeared above reproach. A dedicated public servant admired for his sincerity, for his sobriety, he'd been easy to recruit. So easy. When his gambling debts had threatened him with exposure and ruin, the consortium, like hyenas around carrion, stepped in. Foliere's debts were paid, and he was ensnared forever.

He was trained as an assassin and then turned loose, his love of gambling transposed to a pastime that fired his adrenaline far more. He was still the perfect public servant, ranging the world for UNESCO and for those seven plotting in Geneva.

Rabbit could read off like a litany the reasons for destroying Sheikh Hikmat and his peace initiatives before the United Nations took them seriously. The consortium was international: seven men representing munitions manufacturers the world over, with billions of dollars in armaments waiting for shipment or on the order pad. Both sides in the Mideast struggles purchased this largess.

Peace meant no profits, no dividends, nothing but peace.

"My only words on the subject," Rabbit said carefully, "are that Fox was overheard discussing his plans."

"Discussing them with whom?"

"I've no idea."

"I see." A long pause filled with faint sounds of crackling traversed the bundle of glass wires. "And now Fox is gone, but someone unknown is carrying that information around with him."

"Not quite unknown; not quite," Rabbit said. Her, not him. Marti Holland, the conduit. "I said he was overheard. We know the party that overheard the Fox." They had followed Foliere to the Waldorf, had heard him ask for Gideon Sanders's room. Had followed him up and in the quiet corridor had overtaken him and questioned him.

"Whom were you with this evening in the delegates' lounge at the United Nations?"

"What are you talking about? I wasn't anywhere near the delegates' lounge today."

At first Foliere wasn't frightened. He was, in fact, very sure of himself. His lip had curled disdainfully. It was Rabbit, in fact, who flinched. They had never liked each other, for no other reason than that they shared the same terrible secrets.

"You were overheard talking to someone about the hit."

"You're crazy. I've never talked to anyone."

"You were overheard by Marti Holland."

"Then she's a liar."

"She has absolutely no reason to lie, Foliere."

"Damn you," Foliere had said, his face red with anger. "I was never in the delegates' lounge, and I never talked to anyone. Do you think I'm a fool?"

No, they didn't think he was a fool, but some malfunction had occurred. He had sealed his doom then and there.

Marti Holland would have to die, and perhaps Gideon Sanders would have to die. But care had to be taken. Marti Holland must not be frightened into revealing what she knew to anyone but Rabbit. What she knew had to be given up, and soon—the information offered to a solicitous friend, easily, even in innocence. It could be done. As for the Israeli, one would have to find out his game. It was possible he was a dangerous opponent.

Bear was curious now, and wary. "And what have you done with this party? The one who overheard? Time is short. We'll have to send a substitute. If you think you pluck them out of the want ads . . ."

"You won't have to," Rabbit said.

"Really. And what does that mean?"

"We don't need third parties meddling. I've made a decision. I've a tight little organization here," Rabbit said. "I'm right on the scene."

"I don't like it," Bear said. "You're there to organize the various elements, that's all."

"I've been here all along, and I've an equal share in the stake."

"Yes," Bear said in a musing voice, "so you have."

"I sometimes wonder if you remember."

"Perhaps I should have been named Elephant," said the voice coldly, "because I never forget."

"Then ease your mind. I'm handling it personally from this end."

"Find out who Fox talked to. Pronto."

The call was disconnected. For a long while Rabbit sat in the dark, thinking.

"YOUR TURN NOW." The bright-red letters had been scribbled on her hallway mirror with enough pressure to break the lipstick in half.

For an unwitting moment Marti sagged against Gideon's chest, her heart beating heavily. "What is it? What does it mean?"

"Don't you know?" The words were uttered in a frigid, imperious tone.

Marti drew away from him, a look of horror on her face that Gideon detected at once. She felt as disoriented by his remark as though he'd been far rougher. It was enough, however, to galvanize her into action. She raced from room to room, flicking on switches that threw the entire apartment into a blaze of light.

Then she went back into the foyer. The telephone lay on the hall table beneath the mirror and its blood-red message.

"I'm calling the police," she told Gideon, who was at the door, examining the lock.

He turned to her and said in a calm voice, "Put the receiver down, Marti."

"Gideon, don't tell me what to do. For some reason you've decided I'm suspect number one in Foliere's death.

Well, if that's the case, let's get it over with. The police will know what to do about that," she added, looking with distaste at the scribbled message. "And besides, I want to scrub the wretched thing off. I don't want to stay here with it." Someone had been in her apartment, had violated it, and she stood the accused.

She had already tapped out the police emergency number when Gideon wrested the receiver from her hand. "I said to forget it." His hand enclosed her wrist in a tight grip, and for a moment they stood there watching one another, locked in a silent battle of wills.

"Let me go," Marti said, but Gideon's grip only tightened.

"Exactly what do you expect to gain by making that phone call?"

"Everything. Peace of mind, which is something I haven't had one minute of since I first heard you and David—" She stopped, aware of her gaffe.

"First heard David and me what?"

"Nothing." She pulled away from him, surprised at how easily he let her go.

She caught a look of frozen anger on his face, but when he spoke, his voice had an almost painfully reasonable tone.

"Precisely what do you intend to tell the police?"

She was equally careful in her response. "I'm not quite sure it's any affair of yours, is it?"

He smiled, but she saw no laughter in his eyes. He picked up the receiver and handed it to her. She glanced up at the red marks on her mirror and for an instant closed her eyes against them.

"Thank you," she said curtly to Gideon, her hand tightening around the receiver.

"All courtesies due," he responded.

She began to punch out the number again. Then, perhaps because of Gideon's unexpected capitulation, she put the receiver back in its cradle. "I'm merely going to tell them that I came home and found a threatening message on my mirror."

"And?" His expression hadn't changed. He leaned back against the door frame and dug his hands into his pockets. "Let me play devil's advocate, in this case the police. 'Is there a sign of a break-in, miss?'

"Your response: 'No, I don't see any.'

"The policeman at the other end—a very pleasant chap, by the way, with all night to waste: 'Do you live alone, miss?'

"You: 'Yes.'"

"On the contrary," Marti threw in, "I have a room-mate."

Gideon's eyes lit up with interest. "Do you, now? And is she in the habit of scribbling all over your mirror?"

"Are you playing devil's advocate," she asked angrily, "or are you just curious?"

"Oh, either one."

"Gideon, my roommate moved out. It's true she might have misplaced her key one or two times, but she doesn't write threatening notes on mirrors."

"Tell that to the police," he said.

Marti took up the receiver once again. "There's only one thing you haven't explained, and that's why you don't want me to make this phone call."

"Go ahead."

"You seem to think you have expert knowledge of how our police work."

"I make movies. You'd be surprised at the extent of my expert knowledge in any number of areas."

It took several rings before the receiver was picked up at the other end. All the while she and Gideon watched one another, Marti aware of time moving, of the danger that seemed to seep from the corners of the apartment like smoke

'rom a fire. Then Gideon gave an exasperated sigh and disappeared into her tiny kitchen. From where Marti stood, she
could see everything just as she had left it: her lone coffee
cup in the sink, the cabinet doors shut.

"I'd like to report a break-in," she said to the voice that
picked up the call at the other end. "I live on Eighty-ninth
Street just off Second Avenue."

"Anybody hurt, miss?"

"No."

"Was anything taken above the value of two thousand
dollars?"

"I don't know. I'm not sure."

"Were there signs of breaking and entering?"

"No, but that doesn't mean . . ."

"My suggestion," said the voice patiently, "is that you
come in tomorrow morning and report it in person."

"Just a minute," Marti said. "I'd like to file that com-
plaint right now."

"Would you like to give me your name?"

She was silent for so long that the question was repeated:
"Would you like to give me your name?"

"Forget it," she said in a whisper, aware of Gideon
watching her from the kitchen door. She put the receiver
down.

"'Would you like to state your name?'" Gideon remarked. "Was that his next question?"

"I don't want to discuss it with you."

Gideon came back into the foyer and opened the outside
door. "How well do you know your neighbors?" he asked.
He bent down and carefully examined the doorknob and
lock once again. It would have been a mistake to bring in the
police at this time, but he knew that ultimately he had no
right to stop her. The lock showed no signs of forced entry.
If the kid who had come tearing down the stairs had been in

the apartment, the question was why he had bothered to stop and relock it.

"How well do I know my neighbors?" Marti said. "Well enough. There's a retired nurse who's lived here for twenty years. On the other side are two men who own an art gallery and are more interested in each other than in me."

"How long have they lived here?"

"Terry and I were the last to move in." She spoke hurriedly, afraid of giving too much information or not enough.

Gideon stared at the lock. "Not your average, everyday break-in. Someone used a key."

Marti felt a cold brush of fear. "Check again."

"I don't have to."

"No one has a key," she said evenly. "Except Terry and the superintendent."

"We'll get to that in a minute." Gideon moved lightly along the carpeted floor, aware of the utter silence in the apartment. From somewhere in the building he heard the beat of a bass fiddle and drum; someone had a good stereo set.

Beyond the small foyer was the living room, long and narrow, with a fireplace to the left. A glance revealed smart furnishings with all the handsome little touches of someone who traveled and had taste. He prowled the room, suspecting that her callers, if there were more than one, were bent on frightening her more than anything else. The question was why. Nothing seemed out of place. Magazines sat in perfect symmetry on the marble coffee table; the pillows on the couch were plumped but hadn't been used. He checked the windows. The thin-slatted blinds were closed; the pale draperies that framed them, undisturbed. Plants crowded the sill, profusely green leaved and unbroken.

There was one cigarette in the ashtray. Gideon picked it up and showed it to her.

"Yours?"

She shook her head no. "I've no idea whose."

"Not your boyfriend's?"

"I'd have told you," she snapped.

He gave her a long, hard look, the muscles around his mouth tensing.

"Gideon, I'm telling the truth. Stop looking at me as though I'd just stolen the Magna Charta."

He went into one bedroom—her roommate's, he supposed, judging from its unused air. After a quick survey, Gideon came out, touching Marti reassuringly on the arm. He went past her into the back room, Marti's room.

She stayed put in the foyer, wondering what he thought of the way she lived. The African mask on the wall, the commercial but endearing painting of Paris over her bed. The antique quilt bed throw. She listened to the sounds of her closet door being opened and closed, the window blinds drawn up. There was a quick slap as he checked the fire-escape window. It was always kept locked, and for further safety, she had an interior gate across the window.

When he came back, his expression had lost none of its hardness. "Either there's a hell of a lot of coincidence going on here, or you need an armed bodyguard."

Her back arched in anger. "I don't think I need you to tell me how to run my life."

"A warning telephone call, two goons who weren't looking for a friendly card game and now this. A not-so-friendly character comes rushing down the stairs and deliberately knocks you over. A car neither of us noticed waiting for him in front of the building. Blue Pontiac, year unknown. And here a scribbled message on a mirror. A locked door, and except for a cigarette butt and a faint scent of tobacco smoke, no sign that anyone forced his way in."

"My roommate was here, then."

"Is that her lipstick?"

Marti picked it up and looked at it. "It's mine. She never uses this color."

"Does she smoke?"

"She used to."

"But not now."

He ranged the room once or twice and then came back and stood in front of her. "Where is she?"

"Terry? How do I know? I told you, she moved out. She could have come back, but she didn't write that message on the mirror, period. It isn't her writing; it isn't the kind of thing she'd say or do." She stopped. "Your turn now." Was it Terry's way of saying, "Find yourself a Charlie Ray. Your turn now." No, Terry never crowed. It wasn't her hand-writing. Terry would never do it, never. She hadn't been there. Had she?

Marti went into Terry's room, opened the closet door and found Terry's clothes still crammed in. What was gone? She rushed past Gideon into her bedroom and began to check frantically through her closet, which held the overflow of Terry's wardrobe in addition to her own clothes. Nothing missing. It was all there—Terry's clothes crammed in at the back, summer dresses Marti knew only too well. If Terry had come, had taken something away, Marti couldn't for the life of her figure out what it was. She turned and found Gideon coming toward her.

He grasped her shoulders, his face inches from hers. "You know something you're not telling me."

She flinched, feeling the warmth of his breath on her cheek. "Gideon, I'm not playing games with you."

"If you're lying, I'll find out."

"What do you mean you'll find out?" Angrily Marti tore away from him. "What's your role in all this?"

He cursed himself silently for his slip. "Figure of speech. If you want to add a little drama to your life, this is a hel-luva way to do it."

"Gideon, what is the matter with you?" She marched into her living room. There she pulled off her raincoat and threw it on the couch. "My apartment has been violated, damn it, by person or persons unknown. My roommate was not here. I give you my word. My solemn oath. She wasn't here." Marti pushed her coat aside and plopped down on the couch.

"Who else has a key?"

"Nobody." Her answer was sharper than she had intended.

"Really? Think."

"If you mean do I have affairs and give my key to men all over the city," she said hotly, "the answer is no. N dash O."

"Not even one man with one key?"

"The answer is no," she said evenly, "so get off that track."

"This roommate of yours—any chance that a key to the apartment is tucked in someone's wallet, thanks to her?"

"The answer to that is also no. Terry falls in love a devil of a lot, but none of her boyfriends ever bedded down here. That was the rule we made when we took the apartment. Can we get off the subject of my roommate, please?"

"Look," Gideon said, sitting down beside her and taking up both her hands in his, "you're not being disloyal. You've just had a poison-pen letter delivered to you via your foyer mirror. I'd be a bit nervous if I were you."

"I'm more than nervous, Gideon."

"Tell me once more about the phone call this morning."

"The phone call this morning," she reiterated with a sigh. "I told you everything. He didn't seem hurried. Almost friendly, in fact." She glanced at Gideon, her eyes narrowed, trying to remember. "At first, when the phone rang, I thought it was you."

In his eyes she saw an unexpected light of pleased surprise. "I did," she said softly. "I thought it was you."

"Really? What made you think that?"

"I don't know. My secretary said the man wouldn't give his name. Somehow…I don't know, I just thought it would be you."

He watched her, bemused. Could it have been that simple? Marti Holland coming into the Moroccan reception and heading straight for him and David, a butterfly looking for a plant on which to alight? "That's an explanation that's no explanation." He smiled, the lines around his mouth relaxing for the first time since they had left the nightclub.

"I suppose so." Their gaze held for an instant, and suddenly he released her hands and drew her close.

"Marti," he said, "you've got to trust me."

"I see. Suddenly I've got to trust you."

He brushed his hand through her hair and put his lips softly against her forehead. "Truce?"

She relaxed into him, wondering where the line for trust could be drawn. She was too tired to work it out for herself. "Just like that?"

"Marti, just like that. Go on about the telephone call."

"Right. The telephone call." She closed her eyes, her cheek against the roughness of his jacket, feeling the warmth of his arm around her. Truce, trust; what did it matter? She'd have to deal with everything soon, and there was no one to turn to but this man. "Virginia Upson was waiting for me," she began, "dripping sarcasm all over my office. She was in a snit because Foliere's death inconvenienced her greatly. That's Virginia. I picked up the receiver. I had thought it would be you but realized at once that I was mistaken."

"And you don't remember what kind of accent?"

"No. Perhaps the accent was made up. But he sounded quite pleasant. There was a slight laugh in his tone. He wasn't very direct in what he said. Just that they didn't know what I knew but that they knew I knew something."

He put his hand under her chin and turned her face toward him. "I couldn't have put it better myself."

He felt a shiver race through her body and pulled her closer. "Start at the beginning, Marti, the very, very beginning."

What a fool he was acting, he berated himself. He wanted to believe she was caught accidentally in something she didn't understand. To believe it and throw caution to the wind. Even risk being wrong about her. Damn, there was too much at stake for him to be taken in. If there was a plot against Sheikh Hikmat's life, experience told him not to discount Marti Holland. What he had to know was whether or not she was a willing participant in it. She had heard him talking to David Lund. Where? And about what?

"The very, very beginning," she murmured. "Oh, heavens, that was a million years ago."

"Don't be afraid," he whispered against her ear. "I won't let anything hurt you." He buried his face in her hair and once again inhaled the fragrance of that elusive desert flower. He had always despised men who, when they were caught in the act of betraying their ideals, blamed a beautiful woman for their downfall. Now, although he still believed himself strong, he could understand their weakness. She was hard to resist, Marti Holland. He brushed the thought away and said more gruffly than he had intended, "Who owns this building?"

She shrugged. "New York and Suburban Properties. Faceless. I send a check out each month."

"Who's the concierge?"

"This not being Paris, we have a major domo in the form of a stout, good-hearted widow who lives in the basement apartment."

"Does she have a key to the apartment?"

"Certainly."

He looked into her eyes and then shook his head wonderingly at the absolute trust she placed in the honesty of the lady who took her mail and came in to water the plants when she was out of town. "Has she a son, a daughter?"

"Her son in California runs a rather successful carwashing operation; her daughter lives upstate on a farm."

Releasing her, he stood up and began to prowl the room. "What else can you tell me?"

"About what, for heaven's sake? Gideon, sit down, you're making me nervous."

He stopped at the small Queen Anne desk in the corner and picked up the gold-framed picture of her parents, taken fifteen years earlier at Cape Cod. "Your father's smile, your mother's eyes," he pronounced after a few moments. "How about scaring up a cup of tea? This is going to be a long night."

She nodded, took herself off the couch and went into the kitchen.

"Gideon," she called, "how do you take your tea?"

"Milk, two teaspoons of sugar."

"Milk, sugar, then. Gideon, are you messing around my desk? There's nothing there that should concern you."

"What gave you that idea?" He came to the door of the kitchen and leaned against the wall. He gazed at her as if he were trying to connect the dots and form a whole picture. "Have you told me absolutely everything about Jacques Foliere and you?"

"Yes," she snapped. "Unless you want a rundown of where he was born and how he came to work for UNESCO. Only," she added with a smile, "I've no idea about him except that he was born in the Auvergne."

"When you were talking, did he seem agitated or in a hurry?"

She filled the kettle with water and set it carefully on the stove. "Neither. A man with some time on his hands." She hadn't paid much attention to Foliere. In fact, she was more annoyed with him than anything else. It was because of him that she'd lost sight of Gideon. She had listened to what Foliere had to say with half an ear. It was Gideon she wondered about, Gideon she hoped would return. Later she brushed aside Foliere's offer of a drink because she wanted to see the chief of security. Jacques Foliere had crossed her line of sight for a little while, and she had thought no more about him.

Gideon, watching her at the stove, hoped the tea would be strong and that she didn't use those insipid little bags filled with bits and pieces of unremarkable leaves.

"Ceylon," she said, pulling down a canister and opening it.

"You're a treasure," he said, smiling at her.

"What's that supposed to mean?"

"Fresh tea."

He realized that he was feeling uncertain for the first time in his life. He had always trusted his instincts about people and was rarely proved wrong. Marti Holland, however, was an enigma. She was afraid but in control, although in her pliable body he had found a whisper of readiness at his touch. Still, Mata Haris these days came well equipped and trained.

As for Foliere, he and David Lund had already gone over the possibilities concerning her. She might have followed Foliere to the Waldorf, accosted him in the fifteenth-floor corridor and put a gun to his head. She needed someone with her, of course, someone strong enough to push Foliere to his death.

In point of fact, it was he, Gideon Sanders, who was responsible for Foliere's manner of dying. After leaving David's apartment, Gideon had called Foliere and invited him to come by later for a drink. Foliere mentioned having an appointment at nine, but he seemed interested in meeting

Gideon. Gideon suggested he could come by any time between ten and midnight, assuring him that he would be back from his dinner date at Regine's and probably in need of a good stiff drink. Foliere readily agreed.

Gideon had had a lot of work to do, and it was shortly after midnight when Foliere had phoned him from the hotel lobby. Gideon found that he was annoyed at the interruption, but he told the diplomat to come up. He remained at his desk and once again became engrossed in his work, losing track of time.

It was perhaps an hour later when he heard a commotion outside his door. He opened it to find his neighbors clustered at the open corridor window, engaging in a whirlwind of speculation and gossip. Gideon quickly learned that a man had fallen to his death and was lying in the street below. The thought that the man could be Foliere caused him some anxiety. The Frenchman hadn't come to see him, after all. What had gone on in the last hour?

It was nearly two in the morning when the police got around to interviewing Gideon. He knew nothing; he had seen nothing and heard nothing. He'd barely escaped behind his door before the photographers arrived on the scene.

Gideon was trying now to tie in Marti with Foliere and Foliere with a possible assassination attempt on Sheikh Hikmat. So far nothing added up, but the thread was there even if he couldn't find the spool. The slip of paper he'd removed from Marti's desk and slipped in his pocket, however, was interesting and very possibly a clue.

Sheikh Hikmat's schedule. One fact stood in Marti's favor. She hadn't hidden it and therefore might not understand what it meant. Either she was someone's dupe or the best actress since Sarah Bernhardt.

"You can't stay here for the night," he told Marti at last. "That warning on the mirror may be part of a series of attempts to scare you into revealing what you know."

She set two cups on a white doily she had placed on the tea tray. He smiled almost involuntarily. It was funny what a woman would think of even in a moment of crisis.

"I'm not sure what you mean," she said carefully. "They're trying slowly and inexorably to scare the pants off me. If I'm scared enough, I won't run to the police with what I know, except I don't know what I know." The very statement threw her into a paroxysm of action.

"I'm going to call Terry and ask her to put me up for the night. Or Virginia Upson." She stopped, frowned and gritted her teeth. It wouldn't be asking Terry; it would be asking Charlie Ray, and somehow that didn't seem right. As for Virginia, it was past midnight, and if true to her schedule, Virginia would have been fast asleep at ten o'clock on the button. "I've a friend in Westchester," she said lamely.

"My suite at the Waldorf?" Gideon asked, smiling.

"That's the last place you'd see me."

"I thought so."

"Gideon, you don't have to tell me not to stay here tonight. There's no way I'd do it."

"Look, there's an easy solution to this problem if you just give me a moment or two." Once the tea was poured, he took the tray from her and carried it into the living room.

"A moment or two," she echoed, frowning at him.

They sat down on the couch. After his first scalding sip of tea, Gideon turned toward her. "Marti, I'm not going to let anything happen to you. I told you that, and I've never been more serious."

As he pulled her close, Marti felt the warm strength of his arms enfolding her. There was a new tenderness in the way he held her, mingled with a fierce determination that made her realize that getting away from him wouldn't be easy. Her arms went around him as naturally as if they'd been together for years.

"Gideon…" she began, only to be silenced when his lips found hers. The touch was hurried and compelling and so unexpected she found herself trying to tear away. His grip tightened, and Marti knew she didn't really want to run. She needed him, needed his comfort and certainty. She murmured his name once again as he gently pried open her lips with his tongue.

"Hush," he whispered. A low moan of pleasure came from one of them, but Marti couldn't have said which. And then a swift, surprising savagery, an intensity to his kiss that startled her. His tongue dipped slowly into her mouth, and she found herself responding with her own. For a long moment the events of the day were lost as they savored one another. His hand left her waist and trailed slowly up to circle her breast with a soft pressure. He moved his mouth to her throat. As a slow heat warmed her body, she lifted her head to give him easy access.

He took her mouth again, grinding his lips against hers with an explosive release of pent-up longing. Then, just as suddenly as it had begun, it ended. Gideon pushed her away, muttering a mild expletive as he pounded his fist into his hand. Marti stifled a light cry. He turned toward her and gathered her in his arms.

"I'm sorry," he told her softly. "All you need now is someone pawing at you."

"Gideon, I didn't stop you," she murmured.

"That's because you're scared." He tilted her chin and gazed at her, and they both knew it wasn't true.

He had lusted after women before, but he had never fooled himself that it was anything else. Marti was different. With her, he was acting on intuition, casting aside all his training and experience. It might, he thought with an inward laugh, just have him killed even before he was able to complete his assignment.

"Gideon," she said, "I'll call my friend in Westchester."

He was a long time answering. "Go ahead," he said finally, "if you want to. Does she have a husband? Children?"

A cold prickle of fear erupted along her spine. "Yes."

"I do have a suggestion," he told her. It had been there at the back of his mind. Pilar do Valles. Keep Marti hidden in plain sight at Pilar's apartment, where there were servants and guests and that terrible dog.

"A hotel?" she asked.

"Besides my room at the Waldorf? Pilar do Valles has a large apartment, plenty of people around and a keen eye for drama."

Marti shook her head slowly. "I had the impression she wasn't too crazy about me."

"There's something to be said for narcissism, Marti. Pilar thrives on intrigue, but if something doesn't concern her directly, she won't even ask any questions. As for the impression you had, Pilar thinks every pretty woman in the world is competition. Consider yourself flattered and don't worry about anything else."

They gazed at one another, each wondering about the moment that had just passed and where it might have led them. Gideon tilted her chin. Pushing her away had been one of the hardest things he had ever done, and possibly the smartest.

"Don't worry," he said close to her mouth. "If you do other things as well as you kiss, I'm going to want to keep you safe and sound just to find out."

He let her go reluctantly as he headed for the phone and for what he hoped would be safety.

Chapter Seven

"I never thought I'd be so happy to close that door behind me," Marti said when they were out on the street, waiting for a cab. She had hurriedly packed an overnight bag with essentials for the next day and left quickly, before she could change her mind. Now she turned and glanced regretfully at her fourth-floor living room window. It presented a blank view to the world. Marti wondered if she would ever be able to gaze at it again with a feeling of wanting to be home and tucked inside.

"I'll have to do something about the lock first thing in the morning," she told Gideon.

"Time to talk about all that later," he replied. "Come on; we won't pick up a cab here on the side street." He started at a rapid pace for Second Avenue.

"Gideon." Marti caught up to him and pulled at his sleeve. "If they wanted me to go into hiding, they've made their point. Therefore, they couldn't mean me any actual harm."

He frowned at her. "Don't try to second-guess them. They want you to keep away from the cops, to keep away from the press, and it might be they're trying to fatten you up for the kill."

"I'm not quite sure what you mean," she said.

"Do you know the game of good cop, bad cop?"

"Yes." She nodded. "When you're arrested, one cop is so mean to you that you readily tell your story to the other one, the smiling one. Let me see your teeth, Gideon. I want to check them for sharpness."

"I'm not the good cop, and I'm not the bad one, either. But someone out there may just be waiting for you to run scared."

"Run scared and look for a confidante, is that it? Tell everything I know to someone who's acting like my best friend? Except I don't know anything."

"They don't know you don't know anything."

"Gideon, the only one who's my current confidante is you. I should be scared of you, then."

"Go ahead," he told her with a smile. " 'Scared' is the operative word for the moment. Let's go. I don't like discussions in the middle of the night, in the middle of the street."

"I'd like to stop for a newspaper. Maybe Foliere's killer has been caught and the whole thing is over with. I feel as if the last five or six hours of my life have taken place on the moon."

She realized she had pronounced the French diplomat's name with a kind of reluctance borne of guilt. What if she had gone with him, if only for a little while? If they'd sat somewhere over coffee and chatted on about the pilot project in the Sudan, she might have learned something about the man. Might have kept him busy and away from the Waldorf. Away from— She shivered. Gideon?

"Where are we supposed to find a newspaper?" Gideon was asking. "No, don't tell me; this is New York, which prides itself on never going to sleep."

"There's an all-night general store over on Second Avenue," Marti said. "They have groceries, newspapers, magazines, hot coffee, whatever. Also a huge tabby cat that goes by the name of Roxie. Where does your friend Pilar live?"

"East Fifty-seventh Street. She's borrowing a friend's apartment for the duration."

Marti stopped and frowned at him. "Borrowed apartment? You didn't tell me that."

"I'm telling you now. A very nice borrowed apartment with plenty of rooms for people who suddenly find themselves in need of a place to lie down."

It put a new light on staying at Pilar's. She hadn't been happy about it to begin with, but her only other choices would have been to call Terry and move in with her and Charlie Ray or to call Virginia. Neither one seemed like a good idea. Most of her other friends in the city had tiny efficiency apartments with scarcely room for themselves. Or they were living in small apartments with their lovers. Her alternative was a hotel, and the idea began to sound better and better.

"Oh," she groaned, "why didn't I get home earlier? I could've found someone who'd take in a poor, bedraggled kitten, namely me. I'm not without friends, you know."

"If you'd come home earlier, you might have run into your friends with the lipstick," he countered caustically.

"Gideon, I'm not crazy about staying with Pilar, but now that I know she's living in a borrowed apartment . . ." She made a face, not bothering to finish the sentence.

"What's your alternative?" he asked.

"A hotel. And I'll call my friend in Westchester tomorrow."

"The one with the children?" The question was asked in a quiet, deadly voice.

She was a long time answering. "Yes."

"You'll be safer with Pilar," he told her. "And so will your friend in Westchester. We went through that already."

"Why will I be safer with Pilar?" She glanced around at the nearly empty street, lit to a bluish white at intervals by sodium lamps. But they weren't necessarily safe. The

brownstones that lined the street could hold shadowy figures in hiding behind jutting staircases. She gave an involuntary shiver and pulled her raincoat close.

"Pilar is never alone," Gideon was saying. "She abhors
an empty room. Our man with the lipstick—"

"Or woman," Marti threw in.

"Or woman with the lipstick won't risk getting to you
where he or she might have an audience. As you so cleverly
deduced, Marti," he said with utter seriousness, "if they
wanted to kill you, you'd be dead already."

"Cold comfort," she said. "I can't believe this is happening to me."

He took her arm and led her firmly toward Second Avenue. "A while ago I had the distinct impression that you
were pleased with the idea of staying with Pilar."

"I was never pleased," Marti said. "It just seemed like
the best idea at the time."

"It still is." His answer was terse, and she could tell from
his tone that he had every intention of keeping a close eye on
her.

"You forced me on Pilar," she said truculently. "I heard
her barking over the wire."

He laughed spontaneously and put his arm around her,
hugging her close. "Marti Holland, you're obviously too
clever, too self-sufficient and entirely too modest. Pilar even
barks at her dog—a rather nasty little Pekingese, by the
way—but fortunately the beggar barks back. What you're
going to do with Pilar is charm her in precisely the way you
set about charming David and me at the Moroccan reception yesterday."

"Is that what I did? Set about charming you? Funny, I
don't remember it that way." She pulled closer to him,
needing his warmth and feeling measurably better for it.

"You don't? And precisely what do you remember?"

"I saw two attractive men standing at the window and said to myself, 'No, no, no, that's not the way it should be. Too much symmetry. What we need is the feminine gender. Three's a good crowd in a good crowd'—that sort of thing. I decided to do my patriotic duty. Make you feel at home in my bailiwick."

His arm tightened around her. "What an enchanting little liar you are, Marti. Your bailiwick, is it? But then, of course, you know the building inside and out, don't you?"

She pulled away, but he drew her quickly back. "Is that what you really think of me, Gideon? That I haven't told you one honest thing about myself?"

His face was close, and there was nothing in his eyes but a glint of interest and curiosity. Still, she had the distinct feeling that she would feel his lips on hers if she let the moment lengthen.

"Gideon," she said quietly, "we're talking words, but what we mean is something far more subtle. Pilar is waiting for us. It's late, and we're keeping her up."

His lips brushed the tip of her nose. "Like the city itself, Pilar never sleeps."

"Gideon."

His mouth found hers in a lingering kiss.

"I thought you said someone could be following us."

"Fine, if he wants to be a voyeur." He laughed. "Best possible thing to happen would be to let him see you have a protector." He turned Marti dutifully away, and with his arm still tight around her shoulders, directed her down the street. She looked back once before they hit the brightly lit avenue. There was no one behind them that she could see.

"Looking for a blue Pontiac?"

"I thought maybe one could be trailing us down the street, but no. Although that doesn't mean anything, either."

"If there is one, we'll shake it long before we get to Pilar's. Now, lesson number one about Pilar," Gideon said. "You have to let her know you're an expert in an area that interests her. So you charm her with your extensive knowledge about the United Nations."

"It doesn't strike me that she's at all interested in the United Nations."

"Ah," Gideon said, "but she is. She wants to finish her picture. *Checkpoint* takes place in part at the United Nations. Our locations scout assured us that the UN would cooperate with us, but our locations scout, it turns out, was on a bender in New York and knew no such thing. You, my little Marti, are hereby nominated as locations scout for *Checkpoint*. You've found it. Convince me why we should shoot the very last scene there."

"I'm not taking the job, Gideon. Are you interested in me and my problems or that building, or are we all tied up somehow?"

"Where's that general store you were talking about?" he asked.

"You're a great subject changer, Gideon. I said no, and that no isn't open to negotiation. Down about three blocks. You can see it from here. The place that's all lit up."

"As I said," Gideon went on quickly, "you must tell Pilar all about the United Nations. Explain the inner workings of the building and—"

"Wait, wait; hold it, Gideon," Marti said. She pulled away from him. "I don't believe I'm hearing you correctly."

"You'll have Pilar eating out of your hand if you just follow Papa Gideon's advice."

"Damn it, I don't want her eating out of my hand. This whole thing is bizarre, crazy and—and—insane. If it weren't for you, Foliere wouldn't be... Oh, forget it," she muttered, storming on ahead, aware of the look of fury that had clouded his eyes at her remark. If she hadn't overheard that ominous statement about Sheikh Hikmat, she might have left the reception early, as she had planned. She might never have run into Virginia, might never have been palmed off on Foliere. Might never have met Gideon Sanders. Might, might, might. The mights stretched in a straight line all the way to the moon.

At the end of the street she stopped, contrite, and waited for Gideon to catch up. "I'm sorry. I didn't mean it the way it sounded. What are we doing together, anyway? I'm all mixed up, Gideon."

He didn't answer her. The look of anger hadn't subsided. They waited in silence for the light to change and a lone car to make its way through the intersection. They continued down the next two streets in silence, Gideon carrying her overnight bag. The store blazed with light, its open-air stands in front filled with bright fruits and vegetables.

"There's the cat," Marti said, pointing to the fat tabby that was curled up in the window. "Roxie."

"Roxie has the right idea. Sleep. Come on, I'll get you your paper, and then we'll have to get a move on." He picked up the early edition of the *Times* and went inside to pay for it. When he came back out, he said, "It's there on the front page." His voice was totally without inflection.

Marti looked at him, rattled. "What's wrong?"

Gideon shook his head and read off the headline: "'Mystery Still Surrounds Death of UN diplomat.'"

"Go on," she said with a sinking heart. Something was wrong, and he was reluctant to tell her.

"There's a subheadline, Marti."

"Come here," she said, impatiently reaching for the paper.

They stood in the light that poured from the store as Marti read aloud: "'Plastic Revolver Found Among Foliere's Effects.'" She stopped, looked up at Gideon, who was reading over her shoulder, and shook her head. "Plastic! What do you suppose that means?"

"That means it won't be detected at airports or—" he paused, then almost whispered the words "—the United Nations."

"Let's not think the unthinkable," she said, and went back to her reading. "There are more unanswered questions than answered ones in the mysterious death early this morning of Jacques Foliere, French diplomat attached to the staff of UNESCO. Foliere plunged to his death from the fifteenth floor of the Waldorf-Astoria at approximately one a.m. Detectives discovered a plastic revolver with a long barrel in his luggage while checking through the studio apartment Foliere was occupying. While city officials have not ruled out the possibility of suicide, they are now looking into Foliere's background for possible motives of murder. A recent arrival in the States, Foliere was living in borrowed quarters.'" Marti looked back at Gideon, who was reading over her shoulder. "'Borrowed.' That's an interesting thread that's been running through this case."

"Case?" Gideon gave her an amused smile. "You're not a detective, Marti, and the less involved you get, the better it's going to be. And incidentally, my innocent one, 'borrowing' apartments is precisely what international travelers do. You have my apartment on the Riviera, and I'll take your Paris flat. Then, when you're in Rio and I'm in New York, we'll switch again—that sort of thing."

"Gideon, you're joking around the subject for my sake. They found a revolver in Foliere's room."

His lips descended for a moment on her cool neck. She leaned back into him and felt his hands grip her shoulders. "He was a diplomat. He traveled the African continent. Diplomats often feel threatened enough to carry weapons."

"Plastic, Gideon. That means he didn't want it discovered by metal-detecting devices, either at airports or the United Nations." She felt his grip tighten for a moment.

"Want to continue with the article, or shall we move on to Pilar's?" he asked.

"You don't want to talk about it. That worries me more, but let's go to Pilar's. We can argue it out there, I guess." She was about to fold up the paper when Virginia Upson's name jumped out at her. "Good heavens, they've interviewed Virginia! Give me a second; I have to read this."

"Virginia Upson," he mused aloud. "The thin, toothy lady who separated us yesterday."

"Head of my department. Quote, 'Virginia Upson, head of the' et cetera, et cetera and so on... Wait a minute, here." Marti went on, her heart sinking: "'Mrs. Upson said that the last person to see Foliere alive was her assistant, Marti Holland, and that the police want to question her.'" She shook her head. "Virginia keeps saying that. How does she know I was the last person to see him alive? Obviously the killer was." She looked sharply back at Gideon, but he presented her with a blank face. Marti resumed reading. "'Mrs. Upson went on to say that although Miss Holland and Foliere had collaborated on a pilot project for the Sudan, they met for the first time last night at a reception at the United Nations.'"

Exasperated, she shoved the newspaper at Gideon. "You know, Virginia is a brilliant economist, but she loves to hear the sound of her own voice. In order to do that, she'll say anything to anyone. The police want to talk to me! Sounds like I'm a fugitive from justice. And then when I call them, they give me the runaround. Gideon..." She looked at him with imploring eyes. "Am I in a great deal of trouble just because I said two words to Jacques Foliere?"

He considered her for a while before answering. "What haven't you told me?"

She flushed and turned away, walking rapidly out to the curb. A cab came by with its light on, and she hailed it. Gideon climbed in beside her and gave Pilar's address.

"Do you suppose we're being followed?" she asked tiredly.

He looked out the rear window. "No occupied cars, no mysterious men or women hailing cabs. I'll keep checking." The cab pulled away from the curb, and Gideon checked the rear and side windows for the space of several blocks. "Unless they've gone invisible, I guess they figured a scare would be enough to keep you quiet."

"It was. What will I tell the police when they catch up with me?"

"The truth, including the call to your precinct. Should get a few people in trouble."

"I don't want that, either."

"You don't want a lot of things, Marti, including answering my question."

"Your question?"

"When are you going to tell me everything?"

She leaned back against the leather seat and looked out the window. "I'm innocent so help me," she said in a voice that she took pains to make light. "There I was minding my own business and the world intruded. That," she added, turning to him and knowing the expression on her face had never been more serious, "is the absolute, unvarnished truth, Gideon. I was simply minding my own business." Minding my own business and wishing it would change, that she could sail away on the currents of the East River to a distant adventure. Wishing for wishes to come true, and so they had come true, along with the police wanting to question her.

He reached over and covered her hand with his. "Marti, when will you learn that I care what happens to you?"

She felt the tears spring to her eyes. She'd lived here, there and everywhere over the last six years. She had friends all over the globe—and no one. Now she was trying to make a life for herself in one place, and she'd been wary, too wary. Suddenly here she was with a stranger asking her for a simple commitment, belief in his caring about her.

"Soon," she said in a soft, barely audible voice.

PILAR'S BORROWED APARTMENT was the penthouse of an old red brick building in Sutton Place. It was handsomely decorated in an Italian rococo style with patterned chinoiserie wallpaper, coromandel screens and gracefully carved furniture. Pilar, however, was clearly a messy guest. Newspapers, magazines and a pair of high-heeled shoes scattered in the oval foyer added to the general sense of disorder that seemed to accompany her like a cloud of gloom.

The Pekingese came barking over to Marti as soon as David Lund pulled open the door. The animal was of a golden color with thick, silken hair and a high-pitched voice that he continued to use while running frantically around Marti's leg.

"Tintin!" Pilar's voice came crying affectionately after the dog from the living room beyond the foyer. "That you, Gideon?"

"Be right with you," Gideon called.

"Here, let me get your things," David said. "I'm playing butler tonight."

"Where's the host?" Gideon asked.

"Franta? Huddling with Alec in the library. I'm bushed," David said. "Alec wants to go over the details of the budget one more time, Gideon. He's afraid this delay at the UN is going to cost him a lot more money than he bargained for."

"I don't recall him bargaining," Gideon said. "We're shooting in two days' time on the Queensborough Bridge.

There won't be any delay. And as for our new locations scout," he added, smiling at Marti, "here she is."

"Alec?" Marti asked, too tired to contest Gideon's remark. "Didn't I meet him at Talley's?"

"You did. He's an outside backer who's also keeping a close watch on finances for the production company," David told her. "Somebody has to do the dirty work." He hung up Marti's coat. Then he took her arm and led her through the foyer into a large, square living room.

"Here's your guest, Pilar," he announced in a hearty voice. "Can I get you something to drink, Marti?"

Marti shook her head no.

Pilar, in a bright-red silk dressing gown that gave her skin a deep luster, was reclining on a pale upholstered couch that faced the fireplace. A fire had been built, casting a soft glow about the beautifully proportioned room.

Upon their entrance, Pilar threw the sheaf of papers she was reading to the floor. She made no effort to get up, however. The dog, in fact, leaped onto the couch and then settled down on her stomach.

"Tintin," she purred, and then smiled sharply at Marti. "I thought perhaps the corner guest room. What's this about being attacked in your own apartment?"

David shunted Marti over to a wing chair and bade her sit down, but it was Gideon sauntering in behind them who answered for her. "You don't listen, Pilar. I said we believe someone has the key to her apartment. Certain misalignments of furniture, et cetera. She doesn't dare stay there until she replaces the lock."

"You're sure it has nothing to do with you, Gideon? I mean, I sometimes think you're entirely too mysterious for your own good."

"I'm the soul of innocence, Pilar. Your problem is that you'd like me by your side night and day, and that can't be. I've a film to direct."

"Ah, is that what you're doing?"

Gideon smiled, as if he were quite charmed at being bested.

Pilar turned then to Marti and assured her in a voice that was a little shrill, "Well, you're quite welcome to stay, of course. Still," she added, smiling at Gideon, "should I be worried that someone will tear into the place with an UZI automatic?" She drew her hand in a caressing pat along the dog's fur.

"Pilar, you could kill with a smile. We haven't any worry about you at all."

She reached for a half-filled glass and asked Marti sweetly, "Would you care for some champagne?"

Marti, who had been sitting on the edge of her chair, her hands folded in her lap, felt as though she were some kind of unwanted excess baggage that no one knew how to get rid of. She was sleepy, distraught and wanted to be alone so that she could sort out the events of the day, but she said to Pilar, just as sweetly, "Well, yes, perhaps I would like some."

It was David who hurriedly served the drink while Pilar, in her abrupt manner, summoned Gideon over to the couch. "Sit here," she commanded, and although the Pekingese growled once or twice, Gideon indulgently sat down at her side.

David came over to Marti and pulled up a footstool. Although Pilar spoke excellent French, even at her customary rapid pace, Marti was only able to catch a word here and there: *demain* and *cinéma* and *le temps* and *le Queensborough Bridge*.

"Want to talk about it?" David Lund was asking her in a pleasant, fatherly tone.

Marti glanced at him. She was interested in hearing Gideon speak French but supposed she'd make a fool of herself if she tried to join the conversation. She took a sip of champagne. It had a dry, elegant taste, and she sat for a moment staring at the fluted crystal glass and the pale liquid within. She didn't like watching Gideon's broad back as he bent toward Pilar.

"What I really want," she told David, catching an amused look in his eyes that went beyond understanding, "is to go to sleep. Any way I might reasonably excuse myself?"

David hesitated for a moment before turning to Pilar. "She's dead on her feet, Pilar," he remarked. "The corner guest room, did you say?"

"Yes, it's quite ready for you, my dear." Pilar laid a restraining hand on Gideon when he made a move to get to his feet. "As for breakfast tomorrow morning, anytime will do. You can ring for the housekeeper. Oh, and incidentally, Gideon—and you, too, David—a cocktail party tomorrow about six. You, too, of course, my dear, and bring anyone you like; the more the merrier. Celebration for the start of filming here in New York."

David turned to Marti. "The nicest thing about Pilar is the way she'll use anything as an excuse for a party."

Gideon laughed. "Our secondary crew has been filming the bridge sequence without her for a week. Tomorrow our star will make her one and only appearance in front of the cameras."

"The most dangerous scene, if you remember," Pilar pointed out.

At that moment, her husband, Franta, came into the room. He seemed surprised to find Marti and Gideon there but came over to greet them warmly. "You can use a double," he reminded his wife. "Gideon said they can do it as a long shot and finish the close-ups in the studio."

"What a male-chauvinist thing to say," Pilar remarked haughtily, looking unexpectedly at Marti for support. "I'm going to do that scene on the bridge, Pilar do Valles, in person."

Franta, reaching for Marti's hand, shook it politely. "Did I hear my wife invite you to her party tomorrow?"

"Yes, thank you," Marti said, having no intention of being there.

"And your boyfriend," Pilar said. "Bring him; please do. And everybody. *Tout le monde.*"

Marti put her glass down while David went to retrieve her overnight bag from the foyer. She was suddenly furious at Gideon for bringing her there, for making her subject to Pilar's scrutiny, and David's, too, for that matter.

"Come on," David said, returning with her bag. "I'll show you the way. Pilar's man is driving one of her guests home, and the housekeeper turned in hours ago."

Gideon stood up quickly, ignoring Pilar's restraining hand on his arm. He took the overnight bag from David and said to Marti, "Come on; I'll see you all nicely tucked in."

Marti flushed, realizing that Pilar was frowning at her and that David was grinning crookedly.

"Pilar, thank you very much for your kindness," she said, going over and shaking the actress's hand.

Pilar, her eye on Gideon, replied in a monotone, "Pleasant dreams."

Gideon ushered Marti out. "Down the hallway to your right," he said.

"You know exactly where you're going," Marti commented before she could stop herself.

"I borrowed the apartment myself a couple of years ago." He opened the door to a room that was papered in a ribbon print, its huge center bed hung with a canopy in a matching fabric. He put down her overnight bag. "I think you're safe enough, Marti, but I don't want you to take any chances. Don't let anyone know you're here, at least until I tell you it's okay. Deal?"

Marti frowned. "Deal? You mean I do as you say and that's it?"

"Marti," he said softly, and reached for her.

She came into his arms and leaned against him. "I feel like Little Orphan Annie."

Gideon laughed as he brushed his lips against her forehead. "Poor Little Orphan Annie."

"About that gun and Foliere..." she began.

"Forget it, Marti. The less you know and the less you think, the safer you'll be."

She sighed. "If only I could believe you."

They stood for a while, quietly entwined, until they heard Pilar call his name.

"Damn," Gideon said.

"That dog's not the only thing she keeps on a leash," Marti said. "Go on, tell me she hasn't a thing for you."

"You're jealous."

"Good night, Gideon."

He put his lips against hers for a long moment. "I'll call you tomorrow."

"I'll be working tomorrow."

"I'll come pick you up at eight and take you there."

"I can get there under my own steam." She opened the door and waited for him to leave.

"I'll pick you up at eight, Marti. Don't argue."

"Thank you," she said quickly. No, she wouldn't argue. She watched him as he walked down the hallway, lean, strong shouldered, with an easy gait. She hated seeing him go, but she couldn't bear being with him in the same room as Pilar.

She closed the door at last and then thought better of it. She opened it again quietly and checked the lock. It was a simple one that could be broken easily, but a lock nonetheless.

"AND WHAT DO YOU THINK of Miss Holland now?" David Lund, lack of sleep rimming his eyes with red, sat in an easy chair across from Gideon, who lay stretched out on his bed. The suite at the Waldorf-Astoria was decorated in a pale, pleasant, sleep-inducing celadon. David still grasped a glass of scotch, half its contents already consumed.

He eyed the twin bed a little enviously, although his own was a short cab ride away. He speculated that he was getting a little too old, a little too rotund, to keep up with the energetic likes of Gideon Sanders.

"Stretch out, then," Gideon offered, although David hadn't said a word. "Be my guest."

"No, thanks. I'll be on my way. I just find your silence on the subject of Marti Holland to be a mite suspicious. Mind making yourself clear?"

"The police are looking for her," Gideon said.

"Now tell me something I don't know. You've got her hidden away, which, once the police find her, will sit very well with the Israeli government."

"She's in plain sight," Gideon said.

"What's your purpose in stopping her from calling the police?"

"I didn't stop her. She stopped herself. I'm merely hoping that when she does see them, she'll keep her mouth shut. Also, there's something she's not telling me; it's something about you and me."

"Any idea what?"

"She trusts me, up to a point. When she walks into her office tomorrow, the police will be waiting for her, I've no doubt. That they haven't caught up with her yet says they're either inept or know for certain she wasn't the last person to see him alive."

"Perhaps you were," David suggested.

Gideon laughed and sat up. "Are you trying to tell me I might have tossed Foliere just for the exercise? I told you I never saw the man."

David shrugged and looked at his watch. "At three in the morning I can hallucinate any number of scenarios."

"Well, he was followed here, all right, and if I wanted to be any more worried than I am, I ought to change hotels, and prónto." Gideon reached for his jacket, which he'd thrown carelessly onto the foot of his bed. He fished around in his pocket for the piece of paper he'd found in Marti's apartment. "Take a look," he said, handing David the sheet.

David made an exaggerated show of opening it out and smoothing it flat. "Sheikh Hikmat's schedule," he said, "from the time he left the Middle East, and his projected progress through Germany, France and England before arriving on these shores. Very nice fodder for anyone who wants to track the man down. Very private, very personal. Where'd you get it?"

"In Marti Holland's apartment."

David's whistle was long and low. "Well, well, well. Does she know you have this little missive?"

"Not yet."

"And what kind of face will she put on it when she discovers it's missing?"

Gideon shook his head but came up with an answer, anyway. "She'll assume her correspondent has it, the one who writes on mirrors."

"It's the real thing, all right," David said. "We had a devil of a time getting hold of Hikmat's schedule. How do you suppose our little assassin managed it?"

"If I knew the answer to that one, I'd know just what to make of her."

"From the way she looked at you tonight, I'd say you've already made a lot of her."

"You've got a mind that could use a little scrubbing, friend David."

"Picking her up tomorrow, taking her to work," David said. "You've given yourself a baby-sitting job, and you've got a movie to make. Pilar may call herself the producer of *Checkpoint*, but Alec is riding herd on expenditures. You've got to finish filming."

"That's what we have assistant directors for," Gideon said. "When the time comes, I'll be available. What worries me is Foliere and that plastic revolver. Someone killed him, but why? Was he sent to take out Sheikh Hikmat?"

"It's no use trying to follow that one up, Gideon."

"Right now I want Marti Holland eating out of my hand for more reasons than one," Gideon said. "She claims she knows the building inside and out. If she's trying to take out Sheikh Hikmat, I'm going to be there ready to stop her. If not, she's the best bet we have to examine that building from the inside out."

"How are you going to accomplish that?" David asked.

"Elementary, my dear Watson. Everyone loves a movie. I'm going to intrigue her with the charms of filmmaking. First priority, invite her to take part in the filming on the bridge as an extra. She'll fall."

"Will she, now?" David asked.

"She'll fall," Gideon said once again. "I'd bet my life on it."

Chapter Eight

Sleep did not come easily to Marti. The guest room turned out to be at the back of the apartment, facing the Queensborough Bridge, two blocks away. The low, rumbling noise of cars over the bridge went on all night long. She lay awake, exhausted, prey to a hundred sensations that crossed and crisscrossed her brain.

Gideon was there, Gideon above all: smooth, protective, his hands holding her, his lips on hers. Burning, sensual, tender—and too soon. *You don't pick up men and overnight have them turn into worried lovers,* she told herself. There was a tie between him and Sheikh Hikmat. There had to be. He was looking for something and believed she was the key.

His apparent freedom of movement also worried her. Movie directors in the midst of a movie were supposed to be directing. If so, where were all the meetings, the toadies, the rush, bustle and fuss that should attend the ritual?

She drew up a deep sigh. Pilar do Valles could possibly be a smoke screen, but if so, she was certainly a very public one. Marti's fantasies became the strange, middle-of-the-night ones that intrude when imagination can disguise itself as an awful reality. For instance, Marti reasoned, if Gideon wanted to keep a close watch on her, he might even have arranged the break-in. He was there to take her in his

arms, become her protector. But no, impossible. He could
have engineered the break-in but not how Marti might re
spond. She believed in free will. She had come to Pilar'
under her own power. Middle-of-the-night fears. Only day
light would dispel them. At last Marti yawned. There wer
no blacks and whites she could count on; there was merel
a huge, fuzzy gray area between.

The Pekingese's barking at the other end of the apart
ment brought her awake at six in the morning. She heard
Pilar's sharp voice, and then there was silence but for th
low drone of traffic over the bridge.

Marti lay in bed fully awake but reluctant to move. She
wanted to be away from the apartment before Pilar made an
appearance, and she had no intention of returning. Still, she
lay idly gazing at the pattern of ribbon stripes and pale blu
flowers that ornamented the wallpaper. The radiator, dis
guised behind a metal grate painted pale blue, sent up an
occasional clanking sound and a faint hiss of steam.

It was warm under the down comforter. Marti knew the
alternative: getting up, going to work and having both Vir
ginia and the police confront her. Virginia especially would
be full of questions and admonitions. "Where were you?
Why did you leave me in the lurch like that yesterday after
the conference meeting? I looked all over for you. I'm sim
ply furious. Really, Marti, I don't know what the devil's
gotten into you."

What the devil's gotten into me, she said to herself, *is
Gideon Sanders.*

Gideon Sanders, who had taken her over lock, stock and
heart. Gideon Sanders, who treated her as though she were
some rare gem he had turned up in a barrel of colored glass.

Why? It was the simplest question in the world to ask—
and the hardest to answer.

Was he a movie director or a member of the Mossad? Was
he in New York to kill Sheikh Hikmat, or was *Checkpoint*

the real reason? It was too coincidental, the theme of the movie and the arrival of the Sheikh. Or was it? A movie wasn't mounted overnight. Films were years in the making: scripting the story, raising the money to pay for the production, scouting for sites.

The sheikh's scheduled appearance at the United Nations hadn't even been announced until recently. His exact schedule was unknown.... She sat up in bed as cold waves of dread washed over her.

The schedule. "I'll try to get to Sheikh Hikmat in Paris," Foliere had said. "He grants audiences wherever he goes. Here's his schedule. If I can't see him, then you try." Foliere had handed the schedule to her at the Moroccan reception. Where was it?

She had taken it and shoved it into her jacket pocket. Meeting the ruler of a small Mideast nation had seemed too improbable. Sheikh Hikmat, of all people. Was it possible she could meet him and tell him what she had heard? She remembered looking long and hard at Foliere, admiring the boldness of his scheme.

But the schedule—what had happened to it? She had come home tired. She had forgotten all about Foliere. Gideon Sanders was on her mind. Gideon, who had disappeared suddenly from the reception—forever, she thought.

According to Virginia Upson, the police were still looking for her. They hadn't come to her office when she was there or to the council room where she'd spent most of her day. Nor were they at her apartment when she arrived home. They hadn't even called her when she was there. They certainly weren't around when her visitor broke in. Either they were being derelict in their duty, or they knew more about Foliere than they were letting on.

Who had access to her apartment besides Terry? Had someone opened the locks with burglars' tools and carefully relocked them on the way out? Had Terry been so careless with her keys?

Her eye was still tracing the delicate ribbon print of the wallpaper when it came to her. Terry had really been at her apartment last night, after all. That was it. She had come to pick up some of her things, something Marti might have forgotten she owned. Perhaps Terry had decided to say hello to a neighbor and slipped the door latch so she could get back in, then forgot to lock the door on her way out. Perhaps she was with someone—Charlie Ray, maybe—who distracted her. Terry, who was careless. Terry, who was thoughtless. Marti reached for the telephone on the table beside her bed. Terry, whom she must call at once.

She remembered Gideon warning her not to tell anyone where she was. *The hell with him,* she thought. It was more a question of whether her hostess would mind. She picked up the receiver and then checked the time. Six-thirty in the morning. She replaced the receiver in its cradle. There would be time to call Terry after seven or see her at work. She was out of bed and in the shower before another minute had passed.

Gideon had said he would come for her at eight. Marti had plenty of time, but it struck her that part of the puzzle was solved. It was Terry, all right, careless Terry, who had inadvertently left the door to her apartment unlatched, ready for the graffiti artist who followed behind.

At seven, Marti realized she couldn't wait to meet Terry at the office. Besides, Terry's job took her all over the city, and she might not be around for the day.

Charlie Ray Hanson's apartment phone number was in her wallet, scribbled on the back of a business card Terry had handed her one day.

CHARLES RAY HANSON
President
TRH INDUSTRIES

The business address and telephone number were in Galveston. He was a long way from home, where, Marti was certain, he'd have a wife and children. Terry, she decided with a sigh, would one day be back on her doorstep. She'd have to say something, and soon.

It was Charlie Ray who answered the phone in his light, pleasant Texas accent.

"Charlie Ray," she said at once, "this is Marti Holland. I'm looking for Terry."

"Hi, honey, how're you doin'?"

"Fine, thank you. Is she there?"

"Been reading about you in the papers. Looks to me like you're a regular fugitive from justice."

"I just found out last night that the police are looking for me. I haven't been hiding, just busy running around. Doing the town, actually," she added.

"As long as you haven't been running away. What do you mean, doin' the town?"

"Running around with the moving-picture crowd," she said gaily, aware of Charlie Ray's charming ability to make her talk and not minding it at all. She could understand Terry's fascination with him.

"Really? Hollywood. I always wanted to be a Hollywood mogul, but I had the old man's business to run."

"This isn't Hollywood, actually. It's international. Pilar do Valles, as a matter of fact. Actually, I'm calling from her apartment."

"Pilar do Valles, the gorgeous Brazilian. Well, I'm a fan of hers."

"You might think differently if you met her face to face," Marti remarked to herself. But they were getting off the subject, and the subject was talking to Terry.

"Is Terry there, Charlie Ray?"

"No, honey, she isn't. Had something to do with a breakfast meeting at the Waldorf."

The Waldorf again. She was getting heartily sick of the Waldorf. "Charlie Ray, have you any idea of her schedule today?"

"We're having dinner tonight; that's all I know. So are you, incidentally."

"What do you mean?"

"I'm extending the invitation to you, Marti, for dinner. How about it? Bring one of your moviemaking pals if you want."

She thought of Gideon. "I'll have to let you know. Besides, Pilar is having a party here."

"Why, we'd love to come," he said, laughing and sounding impressed.

When, she wondered, had she decided to attend? As for bringing Charlie Ray and Terry, well, why not? But still, she hadn't asked her question yet. "Charlie Ray, do you know if Terry was at the apartment last night?"

"Beats me. I had a late meeting, so we didn't get together until after ten. Any trouble?"

"No. Thanks for the invitation, Charlie. I'll let you know later about tonight, okay?"

"Sure thing."

She hung up, but not before she had the feeling that someone was listening in on the extension. She sat for a long while, her face suffused with heat, wondering.

GIDEON ARRIVED at precisely eight o'clock in the morning. He wore a black turtleneck sweater, jeans and a brown tweed jacket, his lapis-blue eyes lighting up when he saw her. He took both her hands in his. "Well, you look bright eyed and very pretty," he said, bending over and kissing her cheek. He smelled of fresh talc and Irish wool.

Marti was dressed in a black jacket over a pleated plaid skirt, the white jabot of her blouse pinned with an heirloom circlet of pearls. She realized how happy she was that he had come for her and how just being with him assuaged any fears about him. There were none, absolutely none.

"Where's the hostess?" he asked. "Did you have breakfast?"

"No to the second," she said, then whispered, "and, to the first, Pilar's still asleep, fortunately. I don't think I could deal with her this morning."

The apartment was still quiet except for an occasional yap from the dog. Franta do Valles had left very early, the housekeeper had told her, but whether it was before or after she had made her telephone call to Charlie Ray, Marti had no way of ascertaining.

She picked up her overnight bag, but Gideon reached for it and put it down. "Stay here another night."

"Gideon, I can't," she said. "It's an imposition on Pilar and her husband. She really doesn't need a guest at this moment in her life, I'm sure. Besides, so much has been going on that I'm all discombobulated."

He smiled. "A very lovely word, and if it's what it sounds like, I'm sorry indeed. However, you're staying overnight." He put his hand on her shoulder and urged her gently toward the door. "Come on; I've got a busy day ahead, and I want to see you safely ensconced in your office and under Virginia's very cheeky care."

She held back. "Gideon, the police will be waiting for me; I know it. If there's something to be afraid of, they'll have to give me protection."

"Leave the bag here." Grabbing her raincoat, he took her arm and marched her out of the apartment. "Come on, tiger, there's something I want to talk to you about. We can do the talking on the way to the office. I might even stand you to a cup of coffee."

They breakfasted in a small diner close to UN headquarters. Marti, who hadn't eaten anything at Pilar's, dove into a pile of eggs. "What did you want to talk to me about?"

Gideon, sitting over coffee and flapjacks, said, "The police, for one. *If* they come to question you. I'd hate to see my favorite economics adviser sitting in a jail cell."

"Jail cell?" She looked at him wide-eyed. "I didn't do anything. I haven't been avoiding the police, and I've a lot to tell them. The truth, for one. The absolute, unvarnished truth about Jacques Foliere and me."

"The truth?" He looked at her sharply. "Something other than what you've already told me?"

She put her fork down, then reached over and laid her hand across his. "The truth, Gideon, which is precisely what I've been telling you all along. I'd appreciate a little of the same from you."

He picked up her hand and held it firmly. "I didn't want you to make that phone call to the police last night, but I didn't see how I could stop you, either."

"Why? What's it to you?" She frowned, feeling her heart beating heavily in her chest.

He continued to watch her but made no effort to answer her question.

"You're not making a movie at all, are you?"

His eyes unexpectedly took on a new light. "Oh, but I am."

"Why are you sitting quietly here with me, then? I thought movies were made at daybreak."

"They are. And at night break, too."

"Why are you sitting with me, then?" she asked once again, and this time waited for his answer.

"While we sit here," he said softly, "the wheels continue to grind. Stunt men, assistant directors, secondary scenes; everything's going along quite smoothly. I prepare the shoots well ahead, and it proceeds along like clockwork. You know, it's like a manufacturing business that clanks night and day, even while the chief operating officer sleeps."

"And there's never a glitch," she said. "The chief sleeps soundly without fear of being awakened because your prop man has a cold or your locations man gets drunk in New York. Or even when a huge glass building decides not to cooperate, for instance."

His face turned serious, his blue eyes diamonds that cut deep and hard. His grip on her hand tightened. "Marti, don't try to second-guess me. You're right in what you've been thinking all along."

She blanched under his gaze but said nothing. Perhaps the truth would hurt, after all.

"Don't try to ask any questions, because I won't answer them. Trust me." He said the last simply, turning her hand over in his and drawing her palm to his lips.

She felt the touch of his lips with little pleasure, only a sense of dread that she had made an utter fool of herself. " 'Trust me.' That's a phrase we keep throwing around as if it were a basketball. What is it you want?" she asked him coldly, withdrawing her hand into her lap.

"For the moment Foliere's death may be nothing more than coincidence. Your involvement with him may be nothing more than coincidence. It may have nothing to do with the arrival in this country of Sheikh Hikmat...." He stopped at her sudden intake of breath. Narrowing his eyes, he watched her with careful detachment. "Is there something you wanted to tell me?"

"What have you got to do with Sheikh Hikmat?"

"Everything and nothing. Marti, when the sheikh arrives in the States, the police are going to mount extra protection for him that will be hard to penetrate."

"But you believe an attempt will be made here to kill him, or is that something you plan to do yourself?"

He stared at her for a long while, neither incredulity nor anger apparent on his face. "Is that what you believe? That

I've been sent here by my government to dispatch Sheikh Hikmat?''

The words came without her trying to prevent them. "Haven't you?"

He shook his head slowly. "Odd, I thought you might be planning the same thing."

"What?" She shouted the word, only to realize immediately that activity in the diner had ceased and everyone was staring at her.

A glint of satisfaction appeared in his eyes. "Let's get out of here. I've got a long day ahead of me. I don't want you lying to the police; I just don't want you embroidering anything, either. Let them do their job and let me do mine. Fair?''

"No," she said. "We haven't settled anything at all, Gideon."

"Yes," he said, "as a matter of fact we have."

"WELL, I THOUGHT you'd flown the coop." Virginia Upson, smiling toothily over her little joke, brought two men along with her into Marti's office.

"Flown the coop?" Marti looked from one to the other, knowing with a sinking heart that they were the police. Her office suddenly seemed overflowing with giants in tan raincoats as she hastened to offer chairs.

Virginia immediately took Marti's chair behind the desk for herself, which left a stepladder for Marti. "These men are from the local precinct, and they've been running all around town looking for you. Lieutenant Springer and Detective Jepson, this is the elusive Marti Holland."

Marti solemnly shook hands with them, protesting Virginia's remarks. "I haven't been hiding. We just haven't made the right connections."

"You weren't home last night," Lieutenant Springer said. He was a tall, good-looking man with wavy white hair and a youthful face.

Marti went over and sat down on the stepladder. "No," she said at last, "I wasn't."

"Could I ask where you were?"

"Certainly. I stayed with Pilar do Valles."

Detective Jepson, who was recording everything she said in a small notebook, looked up. "Pilar?"

"Do Valles. The actress."

"Of course," Virginia said, beaming at her. "I know just who you mean, but how—? Why weren't you home last night when I called?"

Now was the time to tell, Marti thought. The lipstick on her mirror, the telephone calls, the flight to Pilar's.

"If you'll excuse me, Mrs. Upson," the lieutenant said, frowning reprovingly at Virginia. "Miss Holland, the day before yesterday, at the United Nations, you approached a guard and told him that you'd overheard someone threatening to kill Sheikh Hikmat."

"I was wrong," Marti said.

"Then what did you hear?"

"I heard someone say that the sheikh would die at the United Nations as planned. I never heard him say Sheikh Hikmat. I'm afraid I took it for granted that he meant Sheikh Hikmat. I've since realized that all I heard were two men involved in making a movie talking about that movie."

"According to Reed Douglas, who's in charge of security, you were sufficiently worried to talk to him about it. He explained that an international film company, with an Israeli as its director, wanted to use the United Nations to shoot one of its scenes. I assume you accepted his explanation."

"Yes, I did. It made sense to me. In fact, I felt like a fool, making all that fuss over nothing." She looked over to find

Virginia staring crossly at her but derived some satisfaction from having been able to keep her boss in the dark.

"At the Moroccan party, as a matter of fact, the guards observed you talking to Gideon Sanders."

"Gideon Sanders," Virginia breathed, nodding as if all the pieces suddenly fit together.

"Yes, I thought he was the man I heard, and so I went up to him."

"And did he confirm what he'd said?"

"No," Marti replied slowly, "I never got around to asking him." She turned to Virginia. "I was just about to when you came along. Shortly thereafter I left the party with the intention of seeing the chief of security. I figured I'd raised a bit of a fuss and ought to apologize."

"At the time you walked into his office, however, you'd still no idea what Gideon Sanders was up to?"

She felt warmth suffuse her cheeks. "Well, no, but I knew he was a film director and the son of a diplomat."

"And so you deduced that what he'd said had to do with the filming."

"Yes," she said, and then, "no. I didn't deduce anything. I just figured I'd misunderstood, that's all."

The officer's look was hard and penetrating, but when he spoke, it was to change the subject abruptly. "Now, about Jacques Foliere."

She breathed a sigh of relief and launched into her story at once. She wanted no more talk about Gideon Sanders. "I met Foliere for the first time at the Moroccan party. Virginia introduced us. We'd been working on a project for the Sudan, Foliere in Paris and I in New York."

"Had you corresponded?"

"Yes."

"How often?"

"Three or four letters," Marti said. "He was working through UNESCO. Virginia told me about him and suggested that a plan I've been working on might be useful to him. We agreed to meet when he came to New York."

"May I see the letters?"

"Certainly."

She retrieved them quickly from her file. The lieutenant perused the correspondence and then handed the letters back to her.

"Can you shed any light on what happened to Foliere?"

"None whatsoever. I'm sorry. We talked about what interested us both, that's all."

He stood up and reached inside his jacket for a card holder. Removing a business card, he held it out for her. "If you think of anything at all that might help us, I'd appreciate it if you'd call me."

She read the card very carefully, aware of his watchful eyes. "'Lieutenant Dave Springer.' Certainly, if I do, but as I said..." She shrugged. "I really wish there were something."

"Well, think about it." He gave her a friendly smile and shook her hand. "Where did you say Pilar do Valles is staying?"

"I didn't," Marti said, aware of Virginia's sharp intake of breath. "I honestly don't feel I should tell you."

His friendly smile turned shrewd. "You're not on trial, Miss Holland, and you're perfectly within your rights."

When they were gone, Virginia came around the desk. "Well, you're turning out a queer duck, I must say. Pilar do Valles. Why didn't you give out her address?"

"He can find it," Marti said.

"Marti, I don't know what's gotten into you lately," Virginia went on severely. "Why did you run out of the meeting yesterday? I wanted to talk to you."

"Talk away." Marti went back to her desk, picked up her cup of cold coffee and took a sip. "Virginia, we've got to go forward with the pilot project. Foliere's death shouldn't be allowed to stop that. The one thing he did tell me was that Sheikh Hikmat looks very kindly on agrarian projects and that we might get some money out of him.''

"Now, why didn't you tell that to the police?"

"What? That Sheikh Hikmat can be touched for money?"

"Yes." Her reply was sharp and accusing.

"I have the lieutenant's card," Marti said wearily. "If you insist, I'll call him."

"I don't insist anything," Virginia said. "I just want things normal around here. Is there anything you'd like to tell me?"

"I'd like to go ahead with the project, Virginia. I'm going to try to contact Sheikh Hikmat. Do I have your permission?"

For a moment Virginia looked nonplussed, as though she no longer knew what Marti was talking about. Then she walked abruptly to the door. "Yes, just let me know how things are going," she said. "The sooner this business is over with, the better." The door closed softly behind her.

Marti was left wondering once more where she had put the schedule Foliere had given her. She sat for a while thinking and then restlessly rooted through her bag, knowing it wasn't there. No, it was in her apartment somewhere.

At noon, Gideon called her. The background sounds were noisy and familiar. "I'm on the Queensborough Bridge," he shouted. "It's windy, cold and noisy, and I could use some cuddling to keep warm. Want to hop over here?"

"I'm busy, Gideon."

"Did you see the police?"

"Yes. That's what you've really called about, isn't it?"

"And they didn't lock you up?"

"Gideon, I don't find any of this very funny."

"Look," he said, "as far as I can tell, I'm going to be finished around four o'clock. I'll pick you up at your office around four-thirty."

"I work till five," she replied. "This is America, where we work until five."

"I want a tour of that building across the way, Marti."

"Gideon—" But he had already hung up.

Marti had no luck trying to locate Terry and knew that the only way to see her would be to agree to dinner with her and Charlie Ray. She left a message on his answering machine that she'd accept his invitation. When she came back from a meeting with Virginia, there was a message from Charlie Ray to meet them at ten at Le Cirque.

She decided to take up Pilar's invitation to bring friends along. She had no idea if Gideon would be there but knew she wouldn't ask him about it.

Somewhere along the line she'd have to go back to her apartment to change clothes and to see about a new lock. And think twice about giving Terry the key. There was also Sheikh Hikmat's schedule to root around for.

Gideon arrived late at Marti's office, for which she was relieved. She hadn't been happy about giving him a backstage tour of UN headquarters, especially during the General Assembly, when security was so tight.

During the afternoon she'd called a locksmith and agreed to meet him at her apartment at six. "I'm going to be late," she told Gideon when he arrived at five-thirty.

"I'm coming with you. I want that apartment shut up so tight a bad thought couldn't get through." As they rushed downstairs to grab a cab, Marti told Gideon about her date to meet Terry and Charlie Ray at Le Cirque.

"Fine, what time are we meeting them?"

"We?"

"We."

She had trouble hiding the smile of pleasure that lit up he
face. Outside it had turned brisk and cold, and a sharp rive
breeze was stirring things up. It was dusk, a lingering red
tinged dusk that reflected off the windows of the UN head
quarters building. They found a cab almost at once, and
even the traffic, usually heavy at that time of day, wa
moving at a steady pace uptown.

The locksmith arrived at Marti's apartment a few min
utes after they, and Marti rushed to change while Gideon
dealt with him.

It was what she needed, the hot sting of water against he
skin. She felt the tension wash away, replaced by a certain
relief that Gideon had come back with her. She had dreaded
facing the apartment alone, with that red disfigurement o
her mirror. The first thing Gideon had done was take pape
toweling to it with some glass cleaner.

The sound of masculine laughter drifted into her small
bathroom as she toweled herself dry. She wondered wha
story Gideon had concocted for the locksmith's benefit. The
locksmith had probably not even asked. His business was a
growth industry. There was the sound of the lock being tried
several times, and then the door was closed, followed by the
click of the bolt.

"Everything okay?" she called.

"Perfect. He left a set of keys for you and a set for me."

"A set for you? No way."

"That's what I told him, but he insisted."

"Gideon," she called, "you're incorrigible. Meanwhile
help yourself to a drink." The blast of her hair dryer
drowned out his response.

There was something she had wanted to do as soon as she
came in the apartment. For a long moment, it eluded her
Then at last she remembered. The schedule. That was it
Find the schedule. She closed her eyes and tried to imagine
what she had done with it. She remembered the slip of pa

er, remembered glancing at it absentmindedly. There was a neatly typed series of dates, with one underlined in red. Paris, the Plaza Athénée. It was the sheikh's next-to-last stop before flying to the United States for his speech at the United Nations, Foliere had said. "If I can't see him, then you try." Meaning London, she supposed, or when he came to the States.

She had taken the schedule and put it on her desk; that was it! She looked over at her bedroom door. Gideon was alone in the living room. Was it possible? She turned the hair dryer off and thoughtfully put it down. Gideon picking around her desk, perhaps at this minute. Gideon, in whom she'd allowed herself complete faith.

Removing her robe, Marti slipped quickly into a silk chemise. She was still at her bedroom mirror when she heard a light movement at the door. Marti froze. Through the mirror she saw the door open and watched Gideon move inside. She felt a moment of panic, but the expression in his eyes reassured her. They gazed at one another through the mirror. Marti turned slowly and faced him, aware that she should reach for her robe but knowing suddenly, without a doubt, that she would not. All thoughts of the schedule flew out of her mind.

Gideon didn't say a word as his eyes raked over her body, pausing to watch her breasts swell under the near-transparent material as her breathing quickened in response to his gaze.

"I see you decided not to take that drink," she remarked with a breathlessness that was beyond her control.

"It's not a drink I need." There was a huskiness in his tone that she hadn't heard before.

They continued to gaze at each other through another silent moment. Then he held his hand out and said simply, "Marti."

She held a comb in her hand, its teeth biting into her flesh. She let it fall to her feet. She had thought that when the moment came she would say no. She knew now that she had lied to herself. She had never meant to say no to Gideon Sanders.

Whoever he was, whatever his role was in this drama, Marti wanted him, had wanted him from the moment he had turned his clear blue gaze on her. Was it only two days before? It seemed impossible. It didn't matter. None of it mattered.

She went toward him, her steps silent on the patterned rug. He didn't touch her at first. He merely looked into her face, his eyes delivering the question. Marti shook her head yes, and the simple gesture loosed a cascade of emotions.

Gideon reached for her, folding her in his arms as though the moment had been preordained and they had no control over it. When his lips came down on hers, it was with a softness that surprised her, a sweet hesitancy that vanished almost at once. It was replaced by a hot hunger that sent the foundations of her universe crumbling. She knew that nothing would ever be the same again.

His tongue drove against her lips like a velvet sword. She opened her mouth to him, wanting to know him, to taste him. His lips moved over her mouth. She fought an impulse to run her hands over his flesh, to open his shirt and feel his hard warmth against her aching body.

Too soon, she warned herself. She wasn't prepared for the sudden onslaught of emotions and began to draw back.

Gideon sensed her ambivalence. He whispered her name into her mouth and then raised his head to capture her with a sultry gaze. She held her breath, losing herself in the fathomless blue depths that were yet heated by a violent fire.

"Let the world wait," he whispered before he buried his face in her hair. "I've wanted this since the first moment I saw you."

With a tremulous sigh that shook her whole body, she gave into the need that engulfed her. This kiss was different. Her mouth flowered open as the gentle persuasion of his tongue pressed hers, circling, teasing and exploring her mouth until Marti could bear it no longer. She clung to him, certain she would faint if the sweet torment didn't end. She tore her mouth away, pulling in a deep breath and softly calling his name.

Holding her tightly, he lifted her, and with his lips caressing hers, carried her to the bed. Her body, pulsing with arousal, didn't seem to belong to her anymore. She felt the softness of the bedding beneath her body and Gideon, heavy with desire, over her.

With an effort, he pulled his face away from hers and touched her parted lips with the tip of his finger, tracing a line to her throat. Then his lips followed the same route. He touched the pulse that beat erratically at the curve of her shoulder. Her skin was so soft and yielding, his mouth went dry.

Her arms wound around his back, her breasts flattening against his chest. He slipped one careful finger beneath the strap of her chemise and rolled it gently away. His hand paused at the curve of her breast and slowly cupped the soft mound. As he rubbed his thumb against the nipple, there was an audible intake of breath and then a sigh that wrenched his heart. He gazed longingly into her eyes before he began to nuzzle her neck, running a trail of kisses along her flesh and down to her breast. He was gripped by a wave of desire pulsating throughout his body, the familiar urgency of lust mixed with a new, yet unknown desire.

And then he couldn't wait any longer. With practiced fingers he slid the silken material over her body and tossed it to the floor. She was even more beautiful than he had dreamed she would be. She moved a bit as if she wanted to escape his hungry gaze. He laughed as he drew her close and murmured in a gentle voice, "You're lovely; do you know that?"

"I want to be for you." Her breath touched his ear.

"Do you mind the light?"

"No. I should be shy, but with you I'm not."

"I'm glad."

He rose and swiftly removed his own clothes, tossing them in a heap on the floor. As he moved into her open arms, he knew he would have to exercise the most exquisite control to keep from taking her too quickly.

She arched her back at the touch of his hand, ready for him with a hunger he hadn't expected. He poised over her, his eyes locked with hers as he entered a dream that took his breath away.

SHE WAS TUCKED into his arms, her head against his chest, when he opened his eyes. Her breathing was deep and even. The room was bathed in a soft glow. Gideon knew that if there were one moment in his life that he could keep repeating over and over again, this would be it.

She opened her eyes and met his gaze. "I can't believe that really happened," she said, unable to contain a shy smile.

He laughed as he drew her close. "That's quite a compliment." Her body felt warm and damp from their lovemaking.

"I hate to break the spell," she said when he lifted his lips from hers, "but if it's anywhere near the time I think it is, we've missed Terry and Charlie Ray at Le Cirque. They could very well show up at the front door if we're not there."

"We've got a new lock, remember?" He nuzzled her throat, making no attempt to move.

"And Pilar's party, Gideon. Charlie Ray was ecstatic when I said I knew her. He calmly invited himself along to her party."

"Ah," Gideon said, "the aggressive American character, something we Israelis admire to a fault. Who is this Charlie Ray Hanson?"

"A Texas industrialist who's fascinated with movies."

Gideon cocked an eyebrow at her, looking interested. "Is he, now?"

"I guess you're always in the market for a new backer," she said slowly.

"And what is this industrialist so industrious at?"

She shrugged. "Right now, enjoying my roommate, I'd say."

"Well," Gideon remarked, reaching for her once again, "we've got a lot in common, Charlie Ray and I."

Chapter Nine

A call to Le Cirque found Terry and Charlie Ray on their way out of the restaurant. They had already eaten and were planning, as Marti had predicted, to storm her apartment.

"We're meeting at Pilar's," Marti told Gideon when she had hung up. "Come on, move—*vite, vite!* I said we'd be there in a half hour."

"You said it; I didn't," Gideon remarked, yawning luxuriantly and pulling her into his arms. "I'm staying right here."

"Fine," Marti said. "I've no objection at all. My suitcase is at Pilar's. I'll just run over and get it and—"

"You win," he interrupted with a grin. "I'm not letting you out of my sight."

She pressed her lips against his, her eyes filling with unexpected tears. "For political reasons or what?"

"Or what. Come on."

It was nearing eleven o'clock when they arrived at Pilar's building on East Fifty-seventh Street. They were waiting at the elevator when Terry and Charlie Ray sailed through the door hand in hand.

"You missed the most incredible spaghetti primavera," Terry exclaimed without pausing to greet them.

Marti wondered if they both hadn't had too much to drink. "Spaghetti primavera," she remarked. "And to think it isn't even spring."

Terry's light laugh broke off abruptly when she turned toward Gideon. "Hey, hello. You're... Wait, don't tell me." She stared at him for a moment and then said to Marti, "But he's the one from the reception, right? Standing at the window? You pointed him out to me." She stood to one side and checked Gideon's profile. "Well, well, well, that's absolutely right. I never forget a profile, with or without my contact lenses." She extended her hand out and vigorously shook Gideon's. "Marti's mysterious stranger. I'm delighted to meet you, mysterious stranger. Charlie Ray Hanson, this is—" She stopped and looked helplessly at Marti.

"Gideon Sanders," Marti supplied hastily, feeling the beginnings of a blush creep over her. She wondered if the love she and Gideon had made was visible in her eyes. She turned away quickly to avoid Terry's gaze. "Gideon, I'd like you to meet Terry Atwater and Charlie Ray Hanson." Suddenly she had one more problem to contend with. Terry recognized Gideon, and there was no doubt whatsoever that Gideon realized it.

The elevator door opened, and they trooped in.

"Penthouse floor," Gideon said to the operator as Marti retreated to a corner of the elevator. She had unnecessarily complicated matters by not being honest with him. Somehow she'd have to keep him away from Terry. The ride up seemed to take forever. It was only when they reached the penthouse floor that Marti realized she had been holding her breath the entire time.

The party at Pilar's was in full swing. In fact, it had spilled out of the apartment into the corridor. There was a crush of furs and sequins, of tweeds and tuxedos, a clink of glasses and laughter, and a mélange of heady perfumes.

"Had enough?" Gideon inquired almost at once. "Let's go."

"No, not yet." There were too many questions that Gideon would want answered when they were alone, and Marti wasn't prepared for any one of them.

"Gideon!" An aggressive blonde pushed her way past Marti and presented Gideon with a loud kiss on his cheek. "You're the most impossible man who ever lived," she stated.

"Now where did you ever get that idea?" he asked.

"Gideon, you've got to meet Harry," the blonde continued. "Come on; he's been waiting."

Gideon looked over at Marti as if to tell her that the decision to stay had been hers and that she was on her own. "Then we mustn't keep Harry waiting," he said, moving off at once, leaving Marti behind with Terry and Charlie Ray.

Charlie Ray put an encouraging hand on her arm. "Stay put, you and Terry. I'll rustle us up some drinks and then figure out where we go from there."

"Stay put, out here?" Terry called after him. "No way!" But he was gone into the crowd. "The trouble with Charlie Ray," she explained to Marti, "is that he's very much Mr. In Charge."

"Come on," Marti said, shouldering her way into the apartment, "I think I see Pilar's husband over there by the plant stand in the foyer. The man in the brown suit who looks totally lost."

Terry grabbed Marti's coat sleeve. "Try not to lose me. I don't trust Charlie alone in here with all these gorgeous women, and what I mean to do is find him and drag him out at once. And I suggest you do the same. About that hunk," she added, "didn't you tell me something about him? You were looking for him because—"

"That's Franta do Valles," Marti put in hurriedly. "Come on; let's go talk to him." Marti realized at once that

Franta needed rescuing from his own party and felt an unexpected urge to be the one to do it. It struck her that he had garnered a prize when he married Pilar but was no longer certain it was worth the winning. She wondered whether it might be possible to approach do Valles for funding of her Sudan project. She forced down a laugh. Imagine begging for farming funds in this place!

She found herself wondering whether life with Gideon would be a series of such parties, and if so, whether she was ready for it. But that was jumping the gun, wasn't it? She put her hand to her cheek, remembering his flesh next to hers not an hour before.

She was just about to approach do Valles when Alec Keller and David Lund appeared. David spotted Marti and threw her a wink. The three men held a quick conference and then went slowly together to the back of the apartment.

Marti stood quietly by, feeling suddenly adrift. She turned to Terry and said, "Hey, I brought you here. Let's go and have a good time."

"Those eyes," Terry whispered unexpectedly to Marti as they tried to make their way through the crowd to the living room.

Marti turned to her, feeling faintly confused. "What are you talking about?"

"Gideon Sanders. What a beautiful man. And a movie director. Marti, you amaze me. Look at this—Hollywood, show biz, glamorous women, handsome men. Charlie Ray must be out of his mind with pleasure. Did you ever get that problem all straightened out, by the way? With Gideon, I mean?"

"Yes—yes, of course. I like Charlie Ray, incidentally," Marti added, desperate to change the subject. "I'm really awfully sorry about dinner."

"Never mind. Charlie Ray is out to taste all the *haute cuisine* in Manhattan. He's absolutely crazy about *cordon bleu*. Studied cooking in France for a kick a couple of years ago. Anyway, he's gone into the catering business now."

Marti turned to her in surprise. "I thought he was an industrialist."

Terry laughed. "He is. His company picked up a catering service, you see. It serves food to airlines, et cetera. He's got this thing about improving airline food, poor baby. That's an impossible task, if ever I heard one. Anyway," she went on, pressing into the living room with Marti, "he's crazy about movies, but he's a smart operator, if you know what I mean."

"No," Marti said, turning to her with a puzzled look, "I don't know what you mean. Listen, Terry, I want to ask you a question."

"Which is? Have you any idea where we should put our coats?"

Rock music suddenly blasted from the stereo speakers. Above the music they caught fragments of conversation:

"It grossed twenty-five million the first week."

"My agent told me . . ."

"I wasn't about to sign a contract with that slime; no way!"

"The book, the book—it's the pits, I'm telling you."

"I love this sort of thing," Terry told Marti gleefully. "It's so much more fun than those diplomatic receptions we go to where you have to watch everything you say. I'm impressed to pieces, Marti. You've been leading this incredible secret life."

Marti turned to her roommate. Such parties were new to her, too, but she had no intention of admitting it. There was something else on her mind, anyway, something a lot more serious.

"Terry, were you in the apartment yesterday?" she asked.

Terry shook her head and for a moment didn't appear alarmed by the question. "No, but listen, I have to pick up my black-and-white print dress. What's the matter? Is something wrong? Don't tell me there was a break-in! What'd they take of mine?"

"Nothing," Marti told her hastily, hoping to avoid further questions. "Oh, there's Pilar," she cried, finding an opening through the throng and sighting her hostess sitting on the couch near the fireplace, the Pekingese tucked into her arms. "Come on; I'll introduce you." Charlie Ray, she saw, had already pulled up a chair and was bent forward, talking animatedly to Pilar, his handsome face wreathed in a charming smile.

"Obviously Charlie Ray has managed that nicely," Terry said in her ear. "Of course, he adores that woman. Good heavens, she's far skinnier than I'd imagined. Where's Gideon? How'd you manage to let that blonde take him away?"

"I think he managed quite nicely for himself," Marti said. She was glad for the respite, for the opportunity to pull herself together. She'd have to tell Gideon something, perhaps even the truth. The truth was so simple. She closed her eyes for a moment and for the first time realized that the music reverberated off the walls. Bounced like the voice off the window in the diplomats' lounge. "Oh," she groaned, "that music. I can't think."

"Why would you want to think?" Terry remarked. "What I need right now is a cigarette," she added.

"Will a drink do instead?" Gideon came up behind them and put his hand at Marti's waist.

"I don't know," Marti said, relaxing back against him and wondering if she'd merely imagined his anger. "We were edging our way over to say hello to Pilar."

"Are you sure that's what you want to do?"

Marti laughed. "Listen, I've still got my suitcase here."

"What's that?" Terry asked, looking closely at her.

"Come on," Gideon said. "Let's get the honors over with. I see Charlie Ray has already made himself at home."

"What about our coats?" Terry asked again.

"Let me take yours," Gideon offered. "Marti keeps hers on, as we're leaving right away."

"Uh-uh," said Terry. "I think I've a vested interest in getting Charlie Ray out of this place, too."

Charlie Ray stood up quickly at their approach, his eyes twinkling with triumph. Pilar stopped in the midst of a sentence to turn her gaze from Charlie Ray to Gideon. In spite of the crowded room, she had the couch to herself, as though it were a brocade throne.

"Well," Pilar said to Gideon, pointedly ignoring Marti and giving Terry only a cursory glance, "you took your time getting here. Why doesn't somebody turn down that music? Where's my husband?"

"I've been here for hours, Pilar," Gideon said smoothly, bending to kiss her cheek. "I just couldn't make my way through this mob you invited."

She patted the couch. "Come and sit down next to me. I was talking to Charlie Ray about Brazilian cooking. He knows all about *feijoada*."

Charlie Ray offered Terry his seat, and she promptly took it. "I lived in Brazil long enough," he said, "to know a lot more than that."

"Then you know my language, too," Pilar trilled. Immediately she began to rattle off a long story, at which Charlie Ray nodded complacently. He stood behind Terry, his hands on her shoulders.

Gideon took the opportunity to whisper in Marti's ear. "I've collected your suitcase. Let's get out of here."

She looked gratefully at him. His gaze was steady, but behind the warmth she detected the slightest traces of ice. She'd have to face it sooner or later. "Right," she said, feeling a little nervous, "let's go." She smiled across at Pilar. "I never thanked you properly, Pilar."

Pilar put out a hand, which she allowed Marti to shake. "Gideon, about the shoot tomorrow..."

"Tomorrow and tomorrow and tomorrow," he said. "Good night, Pilar."

Charlie Ray gave them a helpless, apologetic grin. "I promised you two dinner," he said.

"We'll take a rain check," Gideon told him as he took Marti's arm and steered her toward the door.

"I think Terry's having a minor fit at my leaving like this," she remarked.

"Let her."

As soon as the elevator doors closed against the noise of the party, Gideon turned to her, but Marti, feeling breathless and knowing she couldn't do a thing about it, put a hand on his arm. "Gideon," she said imploringly, aware that the elevator operator would miss nothing, "we'll have to talk."

"Cheap talk or the expensive kind?"

She didn't try to respond. It was only when they were out on the street and Gideon had hailed a cab that she spoke again. "I can explain everything."

"Can you, now?"

The cab curved over to the sidewalk, and they climbed inside. After Gideon had given her address to the driver, he faced her and asked in a calm voice, "On a scale of truthfulness, one to ten, how will this story rate?"

"Off the top of the scale," she said. "I'm only guilty of the sin of omission."

"At this point in our lives," he said, "that may be the deadliest sin of all." He turned and glanced out the rear window.

"Are you trying to frighten me?" she asked.

"If I have to try," he remarked, settling back against the seat, "then you've either got to be the coolest customer I've ever come across or the silliest."

"Maybe I'm the silliest." She stared straight ahead at the driver's license, subconsciously memorizing his name and number, all the while talking in a low voice. "You want to know what happened from the beginning. I was in the delegates' lounge about six-fifteen on the night of the Moroccan reception. I was sitting quietly in a chair near the window, waiting for Terry. We were planning to attend the reception together. The chair was close to one of those huge interior columns that I presume hold the building up. I had no idea there was anyone at all on the other side of the column. Suddenly I heard the words, spoken in French, 'The sheikh will die at the United Nations precisely as planned.'"

Over the noise of the engine she quite clearly heard Gideon take in a deep breath.

"I was absolutely stunned," she went on. "I couldn't move. I'd no idea where the voice came from. It almost seemed to me to have bounced off the window. I looked around my immediate vicinity but knew that no one sitting nearby could have spoken those words. When I finally managed to pull myself together, I checked the other side of the post and found no one there."

"And then," Gideon declared, interrupting her, "you were galvanized into action, Mademoiselle Detective, tracking down the owner of the remark. Pretty clever hunting." He gave her a smile of admiration. "How'd you do it?"

"It took a little time." The cab stopped for a light, and Marti stared out at the quiet avenue. A solitary man in a raincoat stood at the curb with his dog. "I had a couple of clues, Gideon. It was you, wasn't it? It's always puzzled me that you and David were speaking in French."

She didn't face him but watched the simple, quiet scene outside the cab window.

Gideon's voice retained its calm. "Were we speaking French? I don't remember. Perhaps it was the ambience of the United Nations."

"You speak it quite well," she observed as the cab started up.

"You forget," he said, "I'm a diplomat's son."

"And were you talking about the movie or the reality?"

He reached over and took her hands in his. "Frankly, I was talking about the difficulties encountered in making the movie at the United Nations. Marti, are you going to help me?" His tone was soft and cajoling, the voice of a man used to getting his way with a caress or a sword. She was certain he was at home with either. The message in his eyes, however, the concentration of his gaze, brought back, with a flush of excitement, their moments of love. He was winning this quiet battle, and Marti wasn't even sure what the war was about. She only knew she wanted him again, with a longing that made her weak with desire.

When the cab stopped at Eighty-ninth and Second, Marti stepped quickly out. The cab sped away as they started down the street. "What do you mean," Marti asked, "am I going to help you?"

He stopped and pulled her around to face him. "I want access to UN headquarters. I want to know exactly what avenues an assassin would have at his disposal to kill someone in the building proper, probably the General Assembly hall but perhaps the delegates' lounge if a reception is held there."

Their eyes locked for a long, quiet moment. In the distance she heard the sounds of a fire engine. Somewhere people were having their lives pulled apart, perhaps catastrophically and permanently changed. And here she was with her own drama, and she had no idea whether it was earth-shattering or not.

"You want my help, Gideon. You're asking me to show you the inner workings of the United Nations during the time of year when security is tightest. We've already stopped beating about the bush as far as your reasons are concerned. Now tell me the truth: Is it for the movie or for that other reason?"

There was a slight pause before he answered her. His eyes flickered gently over her face. "For the movie, of course. I don't want you to know anything else, Marti. Was there ever any other reason?"

POLICE BARRICADES, their lights flashing red in the early dark, closed off the upper level of the graceful century-old Queensborough Bridge. Marti stepped out of her cab amid a small crowd of passersby, a tangle of dogs and children and grown-ups talking animatedly as though anticipating an exciting event.

"What's going on?" someone asked. "An accident, or what?"

"They're making a movie."

"Oh, yeah, I think I read about that."

Despite the festive air, nothing of the filming in progress could be seen beyond the barricade. The road leading to the bridge curved up and around a block of small buildings as if holding them in an embrace. It was in the center of the bridge, half a mile away, that the final, terrifying scene of *Checkpoint* would take place.

Marti went over to the policeman at the barricade. "I believe Mr. Sanders is expecting me," she said. "I'm Marti Holland."

He consulted a list of names and then waved her on. "It's a long walk up," he cautioned.